The Wandering Jew's Daughter

The Wandering Jew's Daughter

by
Paul Féval

translated, annotated and introduced by
Brian Stableford

A Black Coat Press Book

Acknowledgements: I am indebted to the London Library, from which I borrowed the various primary and secondary texts used in these translations, and to Bill Russell for his assistance in compiling the notes. I should also like to thank David McDonnell for proofreading the typescript.

English adaptation, introduction and afterword Copyright © 2005 by Brian Stableford.
Cover illustration Copyright © 2005 by Tim Lambon.

Visit our website at www.blackcoatpress.com

Chapter XXX – The Conflagration
Original Illustration by Yan d'Argent
from *The Wandering Jew's Daughter*

Introduction

- *The History of* The Wandering Jew's Daughter:

Paul Féval's account of *La Fille du Juif Errant* (*The Wandering Jew's Daughter*) was originally published in *Le Musée des Familles* in 1864. Jean-Pierre Galvan gives the date as January 1863 in his bibliography in *Paul Féval: Parcours d'une Oeuvre* (2000), but Michel Nathan–who appears actually to have consulted that version–says in his 1987 essay "*La Fille du Juif-Errant*" (in *Paul Féval: Romancier Populaire*, edited by Jean Rohou and Jacques Dugast) that it was in the June 1864 issue. The original title of the nouvelle was *Le Juif-Errant, Conte pour les Grands Enfants* (*The Wandering Jew: A Fairy Tale for Older Children*).

Féval's account of the iconic figure of the Wandering Jew deviated considerably from previous literary versions of the tale in several respects, the most significant being the introduction of the accursed Wanderer's daughter, of whom nothing had ever been said before, as his traveling companion. The most important of the other modifications is his equipment with a contradictory counterpart in the likewise-unprecedented Ozer, one of an unprecedently extensive company of outcast immortals.

As with earlier fantastic motifs he had tackled, therefore–the vampire being the one to which he most frequently returned–Féval seems to have set out with the firm intention of demonstrating his originality and inventiveness. In this case, however, that intention was compounded with complications that had not troubled his dealings with phantoms and vampires, in that the Wandering Jew was a specifically Christian fantasy: a legend in the narrow sense, whose literary deployment could not help but raise issues of faith. Féval was a devout man, although he later became convinced that he had not been nearly devout enough in the phase of his career in which *The Wandering Jew's Daughter* was written.

The situation was further complicated by the fact that both of Féval's chief rivals as writers of serial fiction for French periodicals, Eugène Sue and Alexandre Dumas, had not only written accounts of the Wandering Jew, but had done so in works that were pivotal to their careers, reflective of the utmost heights of their literary ambition: Sue's *Le Juif Errant* (1844-45; tr. as *The Wandering Jew*) and Dumas' incomplete *Isaac Laquedem* (1853). Sue and Dumas had little enough in common, but one matter in which they stood more or less shoulder-to-shoulder was that they were not devout men, and each of them had been eager to deploy the legend in a calculatedly heretical fashion. This, too, had a profound effect on Féval's attitude to the motif and his strategy in dealing with it.

The original version of Féval's story was reprinted under the first of its variant titles as the title-piece of a collection of three novellas, *Le Vicomte Paul*, published by Michel Lévy in 1873. Its subsequent history was shaped by the fact that on June 10, 1876, following a financial catastrophe that reduced him to penury, Féval published a "lettre de conversion" in the *Bulletin du Voeu National*, in which he repented of having written many of his novels, on account of their immorality. He resolved that, in the future, he would write none but conscientiously pious and morally improving works, and that he would begin the work of revising those of his earlier works that could be rewritten to fit this mold. *Le Vicomte Paul* was one of the first that sprang to mind, and Féval produced a new version of it for serialization in the Catholic periodical *Les Veillées des Chaumières* from November 1877 to January 1878. It was this version that first bore the title "*La Fille du Juif Errant.*" The work was swiftly reprinted under the new title, along with one of the other novellas from *Le Vicomte Paul*, as the title-piece of a book issued by Victor Palmé in 1878. This latter volume became the standard edition, reprinted several times thereafter; it is the version used for this translation.

According to Michel Nathan, the two versions of the text are very similar–much more similar, for instance, than the two versions of *Les Compagnons du Silence* (*The Companions of Silence*), whose revised text shrank by more than a quarter as "unsuitable" passages were ruthlessly excised. Far from shrinking, in fact, *The Wandering Jew's Daughter* expanded slightly, by virtue of the insertion of numerous pious exclamations and observations, and the exaggeration of a few anti-Republican passages. The examples Nathan quotes do, however, bear out his assertion that the changes are merely cosmetic. It seems probable that the text recommended it for early recycling precisely because it required hardly any amendment to bring it into line with Féval's new philosophy of procedure.

The Victor Palmé book carries a preface cast in the form of a letter (to Edmond Biré), in which Féval offers an account of the genesis of the story. It builds on an anecdote that Féval often told, about the success of *Les*

Mystères de Londres (*The Mysteries of London*) having turned his head to the extent that he hired a page and bought a horse, which he named *Juif-Errant* after the classic *roman feuilleton* by Eugène Sue.

Féval had observed before that the horse had died after six months, and was buried by the page, but here he adds the claim that, while engaged in this task, the page had related the first part of the story of Vicomte Paul and the Wandering Jew's Daughter to a gardener. The second part, he claims, was told to him at Beléré, near Tours, when he asked why a house there was known as "the Wandering Jew's house." In putting the two together, he adds, he was able to add much background information by courtesy of an eminent doctor, to whom he gave a place in his narrative under the pseudonym of Doctor Lunat. Given the characterization of Doctor Lunat as a prodigious lunatic, one is inclined to suspect that this whole account is a comic fabrication, although Féval presumably did draw on contemporary urban legends in composing the story. There are, however, two things that he was careful not to say in this introduction.

One is that the story is, among other things, an emotional account of the July Revolution of 1830, through which he had lived. The immediate cause of the 1830 Revolution was the replacement of Louis XVIII's successor, Charles X, by the constitutional monarchy of Louis-Philippe. The reason why that change was so important was that it involved the removal of many of the privileges of the old aristocratic order, which the Restoration had put back in place after the catastrophic fall of Napoleon's Empire.

Féval had been against the Revolution at the time, and when he wrote *The Wandering Jew's Daughter*, he considered his opposition to have been fully justified by subsequent events–specifically, the Revolution of 1848 and the emergence from the consequent chaos that prepared the way for Napoleon III's Second Empire.

The reason he avoided mentioning this in his introduction was not that he had any longer to fear Napoleon III's censors–the Second Empire had been destroyed in 1870 following the battle of Sedan–but that he did not want to advertise his political propaganda in advance, especially in a book ostensibly marketed for children.

The second thing that Féval chose not to mention in the introduction to the Palmé volume is that the work had not been so much a spontaneous product as an idle whim, as a parody of, and sarcastic ideological reply to, works that were widely regarded as masterpieces, by other (more successful) feuilletonists. The reason he did not say so is not that he expected his audience–even its younger members–to be ignorant of the fact, but simply because he did not want to give publicity to the two authors he was mocking.

The work needs to be read in both these contexts, as well as the one that Féval actually offered his readers.

• *The Wandering Jew in the* roman feuilleton*:*

Eugène Sue's *The Wandering Jew* helped to cement the reputation of the *roman feuilleton* as a potential circulation-builder for ambitious newspaper proprietors. It followed directly upon the groundbreaking success of *Les Mystères de Paris* (1843; tr. as *The Mysteries of Paris*). These two serials, running in direct competition with Dumas' *Les Trois Mousquetaires* (tr. as *The Three Musketeers*) and *Le Comte de Monte-Cristo* (tr. as *The Count of Monte Cristo*), had formed the fictional arm of the radical side of an ideologically loaded circulation war between popular newspapers.

Sue took care to reproduce within *The Wandering Jew* all the features that had made *The Mysteries of Paris* such a ground-breaking work of popular fiction–its contemporary setting; its cross-sectional portrait of Parisian society; its proto-soap-operatic fusion of melodrama and domestic drama–but he was a man with a reformist political agenda, and he also took care to cash in on his newly-won celebrity by introducing a strong element of political propaganda. It became one of the biggest bestsellers of its era.

Dumas' *Isaac Laquedem* did not fare nearly so well. Begun in the heady years following the Revolution of 1848, it had been rudely interrupted in its serialization following Louis-Napoleon's *coup d'état*, because the nascent Emperor's censors thought it far too blatantly Republican in its sympathies. Like Sue, Dumas was exiled thereafter from Paris, and although he took advantage of an amnesty to return to the French capital, he never picked up the thread of *Isaac Laquedem*. The extant text, reprinted in book form in 1853, only offers tantalizing hints of the nature and extent of the panoramic view of early European history–mythical as well as actual–that Dumas had intended to provide.

Dumas, writing for papers whose position was somewhat to the right of his own, always had to take some care to disguise the extent of his Republican sympathies. Ironically, his own views might have been better suited to the papers in which Sue's serials appeared, although Sue–as a revolutionary socialist–had to take similar care to disguise the extent of his own radicalism.

It was to serve the purposes of this disguise that the symbolic figure of the Wandering Jew was imported into

Sue's text. *The Wandering Jew* attempts to move beyond the quasi-journalistic railing against injustice and misery that embellished *The Mysteries of Paris*, introducing a broader historical perspective in a quasi-allegorical fashion; the predicament of working men throughout history is here represented by the plight of the accursed Wanderer, whereas the particular predicament of women is represented by the parallel figure of Herodias–the wife of Herod, who procured the death of John the Baptist, as related in Matthew 14:3-12.

The feverish prologue of Sue's novel finds these two symbolic characters attempting to come together, having approached the Behring Straits from two different directions; the narrow but uncrossable stretch of water that separates them is symbolic of their eternal frustration. The narrative, which begins in October 1831, tells the stories of a mixed collection of individuals who–although they are mostly unknown to one another– are all related by virtue of being the only living descendants of a man named Renneport, who performed an act of kindness for the Accursed in the distant past. In return for this act, a small sum of money was deposited, which has grown prodigiously in the meantime, thanks to the geometric progression of compound interest. Renneport's heirs have enjoyed mixed fortunes, now ranging from poor working folk through French aristocrats to a Prince of India, but as the novel opens, they have all been summoned to Paris, commanded to gather in the Red Room of No. 3, Rue Saint François, on February 13, 1832, in order to claim their share of the fortune.

Unfortunately, the one heir who knows all about the fortune and his rivals, is a member of the Society of Jesus, whose masters are determined to appropriate all of it. The Jesuits, therefore, set out to prevent the other heirs from reaching the appointed rendezvous by any means that comes to hand, not excluding murder as a last resort. Their endeavors are only partially successful, but when the fateful day arrives, the fortune is not distributed. (Probably because the serial was so successful, Sue had been forbidden to complete the climax.) The claimants are then being commanded to return on June 1, by which time the plot has gone through a second cycle of intrigues and dire threats. Alas, wherever the accursed Wanderer goes, he is dogged by disaster, and the machinations of the Jesuits are further complicated by a cholera epidemic that threatens to devastate the Machiavellian plotters and their victims alike.

Although Herodias briefly appears on stage in order to postpone the climax, the Wandering Jew plays no part in the main story at all; he does not reappear until the epilogue that completes the novel's frame, when he and Herodias are found together, reposing in a rustic arbor, blessing the Lord for the redemption he has finally allowed them. Forgiven their trespasses, they are now allowed to die in peace. They expire proclaiming the conviction that the dawn they are watching will also be the dawn of a new era for the great human family whose fortunes they have been trying (unavailingly) to secure, because women and working men will soon be liberated from their chains of slavery–despite the treasonous efforts of the Church to prevent the realization of the ideals of the Sermon on the Mount.

Dumas presumably read Sue's work, if only to keep an eye on his opposition, and he was never ashamed to appropriate ideas from others for his own purposes. He presumably believed, as Sue did, that the Revolution of 1848 was the liberation to which he and Sue had looked forward. While Sue gave up writing in order to serve in the new administration, Dumas, however, stuck with what he knew best, and set out to write his own Wandering Jew story as a celebration of the eventual but inevitable triumph of Republicanism over despotism. Typically, however, he decided to make use of the Wandering Jew in a fashion clearly distinct from Sue's; his character would be literal rather than symbolic, employing the Accursed Wanderer as an expert witness to history and interpreter of the thorny and twisted path of political progress.

Isaac Laquedem begins in Rome in 1469, outside a tomb on the Via Appia. There, a traveler who has apparently come from Naples encounters the significantly named Napoleone Orsini, the scion of a once-wealthy family fallen on hard times. The traveler tells Orsini about a treasure hidden long ago by Emperor Commodus, and suggests that, if Orsini will accompany him to the limit of his estate–because he cannot pause in his progress–they might perhaps find what Orsini needs and desires. Their consequent adventure forms a prologue to a meeting between the traveler and Pope Paul II in the Palace of Venice, to whom the traveler offers to tell his life-story.

That story begins in Chapters VII-IX, with a history of Jerusalem prior to the birth of Jesus. Chapters X-XXIX are a biography of Jesus, effectively novelizing the gospels, although the story is much embellished, including a lavish account of a three-hour temptation by Satan while Jesus waits in the Garden of Gethsemane and an elaborate account of events in the household of Caiaphas on the eve of the Crucifixion. The curse exacted upon the luckless Isaac Laquedem–whose conversation with the weary and thirsty Jesus is here quite extensive–is visited in Chapter XXVI.

In the chapter following the account of Jesus' resurrection, Isaac meets Apollonius of Tyana, a Pythagorean philosopher contemporary with Jesus–although he reputedly lived much longer–who acquired a posthumous reputation as a magician and miracle-worker, thanks to an extremely fanciful account of his life by Philostratus, who seems to have been intent on establishing him as a rival role model to Jesus in response to the claims made by early Christians.

The next three chapters elaborate one of the most famous tales from Philostratus (repopularized by Robert Burton's *Anatomy of Melancholy*, which version is the basis of John Keats' poem *Lamia*), in which Apollonius' disciple, Clinias of Corinth, is beguiled by a Phoenician witch named Meroé.

As Isaac and Apollonius continue their travels, passing through Greece on their way to Egypt, some of the mythical legendary and historical background of the places they visit is filled in by a series of interpolated tales. They encounter another witch, Canidia, who conjures up phantoms, including that of her predecessor Medea, and their journey becomes progressively more phantasmagoric when they recruit the aid of a sphinx to seek out Prometheus–who tells them his own story, and the Fates, en route to the Tomb of Cleopatra, who is briefly resuscitated.

At this point, alas, the narrative breaks off (at the end of Chapter XLII), thus denying the world what might have been an epoch-making epic fantasy in prose. Presumably, Isaac's adventures with Apollonius would have extended much further, filling in a great deal more mythical history, and then Dumas would have returned his attention to the 14 centuries of history that elapsed between Christ's death and Isaac's meeting with the

Pope–after which the frame-story about Napoleone Orsini would have been concluded.

- *The Background of Féval's Wandering Jew Story:*

Féval clearly had both Sue's and Dumas' models in mind when he set out to write *The Wandering Jew's Daughter*, but he was just as determined to distance his work from both of them as Dumas had been to distance his from Sue's; indeed, one of his primary motives was to ridicule both.

As a royalist, Féval was no more in sympathy with the Republican Dumas than the socialist Sue, and presumably thought that both had fully deserved the exile imposed upon them by Louis-Napoleon, following the *coup d'état* that established him as Emperor Napoleon III. Féval probably did not regret the fact that Dumas never picked up the thread of *Isaac Laquedem* following his return from exile. These two texts by his rival feuilletonists were not, however, the only significant predecessors of Féval's decision to produce his own quasi-allegorical account of the Wandering Jew, nor his decision to couch that account as a parodic comedy. It also needs to be seen in the context of his own career, and particularly the context of his work for *Le Musée des Familles*–a periodical that had been founded in 1833 and lasted until the very last year of the century, folding in 1900.

Féval's first contribution to *Le Musée* was fortuitously timed. *Les Ouvriers de Londres* (*The Workers of London*), serialized in July-September 1848, was a hymn of complaint about the effects of the Industrial Revolution on the British working class, which looked like an attempt to cash in on the sentiments still running high after the February Revolution–and might, indeed, have been one, despite Féval's distaste for Revolutionary politics and the dutiful note advertising that the story had been written before the events of that February.

He did not become a regular contributor to *Le Musée* until 1860, however, when he began a series of novellas with *Le Chevalier Ténèbre* (April-May; tr. and previously published by Black Coat Press as *Knightshade*). It was followed by *La Garde Noire* (May-June 1861), an account of a British regiment staffed by Scottish highlanders, nicknamed the Black Watch; *Le Poisson d'Or* (March-May 1862), a Breton romance based on a folk tale about a miraculous gold fish; *La Reine Margot et la Mousquetaire* (October-November 1862), the novella reprinted alongside *La Fille du Juif Errant* in the Lévy and Palmé volumes (retitled *Le Carnaval des Enfants* in the latter); and "*Francine, ou Le Fil de la Vierge*" (October 1863). Assuming that Nathan's date is correct, *The Wandering Jew's Daughter* concluded the series, although it is probable that more works appeared in *Le Musée* than are identified in Galvan's bibliography.

Although the settings of these stories are varied, the majority of them have several important things in common, including their hospitality to the fantastic and the fact that they mostly seem to have been planned as works for children. Planned is the operative word here, for few modern readers would think *Knightshade* or *The Wandering Jew's Daughter* suitable for children. The latter certainly makes an initial pretense of being a children's story, featuring a juvenile hero doing childish things, but as soon as it switches to the ballroom scene, Féval's satirical tendencies take over and it begins to fill up with jokes and esoteric references that no child would be likely to understand or appreciate. Even the fact that the novella is carved up into so many small chapters is only partly an affectation of its adaptation for reading aloud to children in bite-sized chunks; its satirical purpose is to mirror and mock the extreme length of Sue's *The Wandering Jew* (which has 156 chapters, counting the prologue) and *Isaac Laquedem* (whose full version would surely have more than doubled the 42 chapters of the extant version).

While this sequence of periodical pieces was in progress, Féval also published a collection of four brief *Romans Enfantins* (1862) in volume form, so it appears that he was making a concerted effort at this time to establish himself as a writer of fiction for younger readers. He had experimented with the medium before–he had published "*Le Médecin Bleu*" (*The Blue Doctor*) in *Le Journal des Enfants* as early as 1843–but the market for children's fiction was undergoing a renaissance in the early 1860s that made the field seem much more attractive. *La Semaine des Enfants*, a magazine launched in 1857, was in the process of making the name of the Comtesse de Ségur, the first important specialist French writer of children's fiction, and Pierre-Jules Hetzel–yet another of Napoleon III's exiles–had followed Dumas' example in accepting amnesty and returning to Paris in 1859.

Given Hetzel's political sympathies–like Sue he had thrown himself enthusiastically into post-Revolutionary politics after February 1848–Féval was not about to start writing for him, but he probably felt that Hetzel's re-entry into the field of children's fiction ought not to go unopposed. In his pre-Revolutionary days, as a publisher of four series of *Le Nouveau Magasin des Enfants*, Hetzel had published novellas by pillars of Romanticism like Charles Nodier and Jules Janin, and had obtained new work from George Sand, Paul de Musset and such feuilletonists as Dumas and Léon Gozlan. He showed every sign of picking up where he had left off–although the significance of his discovery of Jules Verne in 1863 was presumably not immediately apparent to Féval or anyone else. Still, Féval must have realized that the whole context of children's literature had changed by the time the Victor Palmé edition of *The Wandering Jew's Daughter* was published in 1878, still maintaining the half-hearted pretense of being a children's book.

It cannot be claimed that Féval was an effective children's writer, if he qualifies as one at all, but the fact that he made the effort is significant, if only because it substantially increased his interest in the fantastic, which he obviously considered more appropriate to such work. Had he not had it in mind at least to attempt to make them more attractive to children, *Knightshade* and *The Wandering Jew's Daughter* might not have been allowed such free imaginative rein. In retrospect, it is that exceptionally free rein that now makes them particularly interesting to modern readers.

These two novellas are, in a sense, companion-pieces. The former is set on the eve of the July Revolution of 1830, while the second part of the latter is set in Paris during the opening days of that event. The former begins with a grand soirée set in Parisian high society, attended by real historical personages who do not realize that their era is about to end, while the first part of the latter begins with a provincial soirée attended by wholly fictitious characters who can only hope that their arriviste careers will make progress (as, of course, they do, and spectacularly). Both novellas employ exemplary fantastic characters to move their plots forward and–more importantly–to symbolize eternal and irresistible e importantly–to symbolize eternal and irresistible historical forces. Although the eponymous Chevalier and his brother are both evil, while the two principal Wandering Jews are moral opposites, all four characters may be reckoned as incarnations of deadly sins–and the fact that only one of them is repentant is the key difference between the implications of the two works. Both novellas employ aspects of what Féval called, in the former example "the Galland method," having the characters tell tales-within-tales, freely indulging in fantasy as they do so.

In *Knightshade*, the eponymous supernatural brigand and his vampiric brother–who always return, no matter how many times they are killed off–are, to some extent, symbolic embodiments of the ultimately irrepressible forces of destruction that doomed the old Monarchy and paved the way for the subsequent Revolution of 1848. That Revolution, in its turn, prepared the ground for the Second Empire, under which régime Féval wrote both *Knightshade* and *The Wandering Jew's Daughter*. The equivalent of the brothers Ténèbre in *The Wandering Jew's Daughter* is Ozer, who hijacks one body after another, perennially intent on finding positions of political influence whenever the opportunity arises, as well as indulging himself in every sinful dissipation known to man. In the earlier novella, however, the forces of destruction are unopposable–as they have to be, given that the story ends before the Revolution such as they will precipitate. In the latter, which ends in the Revolution's aftermath, the implication is rather different–but the Wandering Jew's torment is still fated to continue, just as history had repeated itself again in and after 1848.

All of these parallels and contrasts are, of course, intentional; on the other hand, both novellas also show the involuntary effects of Féval's invariable make-it-up-as-you-go method of composition, despite their relatively short length. Neither one ends up where it initially seemed to be heading, and the number of loose plot-threads left dangling is profuse in each case. Even readers who cannot reckon this untidiness as an aspect of Féval's ineffable charm, however, will find much in the works that is striking, not merely because they are so highly imaginative and so blithely sarcastic, but because of the depth of feeling simmering away beneath their gaudy surfaces.

Both *Knightshade* and *The Wandering Jew's Daughter* are pioneering exercises in metafiction–self-conscious fabulations whose true subject-matter is the fictions they are reflecting, augmenting and transfiguring–written more than a century before the advent of postmodernism made adventures in metafiction *de rigueur*, and they deserve congratulation for the convolution as well as the sheer exuberance of their calculated craziness. Neither is as good in this respect as *La Ville Vampire* (tr. and published by Black Coat Press as *Vampire City*)–which was probably written a few years afterwards in 1867, although Galvan has not traced any periodical publication prior to its appearance as a book in 1875–but they undoubtedly prepared the way for that endeavor. By filling in the gap between *Knightshade* and *Vampire City*, this translation of *The Wandering Jew's Daughter* will add considerably to the appreciation of those works' achievements.

- *The Legend of the Wandering Jew:*

George K. Anderson's magisterially comprehensive account of *The Legend of the Wandering Jew* (Brown University Press, 1965) informs us that the legend was first written down in the 13th century; how long it had flourished as an item of oral tradition before then we can only guess. Anderson points out, however, that there are older legends with which it has certain elements in common, and from which it may have evolved. The idea that eternal restlessness might be inflicted as punishment for an offense against divine dignity is one a whole series of imagined "tedious afflictions;" the most familiar example is the sentence passed upon Sisyphus in classical mythology, which required him to roll a rock up a hill, starting over every time he lost control and had to watch it roll back down again.

Examples of Accursed Wanderers appear in both Judaeo-Christian and Islamic mythology. The story of Cain, who is sent into exile bearing a mark that identifies him as a murderer, is told in the fourth chapter of Genesis, while the 20th chapter of the Quran (which runs parallel to the 32nd chapter of Exodus) tells the story of Al-Sameri, the maker of the golden calf that lured the followers of Moses to apostasy, who is similarly cursed by the prophet. In neither of these cases, is it explicitly stated that the sinners will be made immortal in order to suffer longer than a normal lifetime would permit, but it would have been easy enough for anyone familiar with the eternally tedious punishments inflicted in the Greek Underworld to take that inference.

The gospels of the New Testament are, of course, far more preoccupied with the idea of immortality than the older writings they set out to overlay with a new faith, and there are passages in them that can be taken to imply that Jesus may have decreed that certain individuals would not die until he returned. In Matthew 16:28, Jesus is reported to have said to his disciples: "Verily I say unto you, There be some standing here, which shall not taste of death, till they see the Son of Man coming in his Kingdom." How literally this is to be construed is a matter for theological argument, but it can certainly be read as a promise of earthly immortality if one accepts that Jesus did not expect to his Kingdom to come for a long time.

Another passage of some significance occurs in John 21:20-22, when Peter, having heard "the disciple whom Jesus loved" (i.e., John) ask Jesus who would betray him, adds "And what shall this man do?" Jesus replies: "If I will that he tarry till I come, what is that to thee? Follow thou me." The next verse comments that the disciples took this to mean that John would not die, but emphasizes that this is by no means the only way of interpreting what was said. Even if one leaves out the obvious supposition that Jesus was speaking purely hypothetically, it is not entirely clear that Peter's "this man" and Jesus' "he" refer to John and not to the betrayer Judas—and there are some accounts of the Wandering Jew which assume that he is indeed Judas. On the other hand, this is the last incident that occurs in the gospel of St. John, and it seems to be included as a way of establishing the credentials of the writer, so it is not surprising that some readers felt that John's own cautionary rider in verse 23 was simple coyness.

There is another story, related in all four gospels, which might also be a contributor to the legend that was eventually written down in the 13th century. When the mob sent by the chief priests comes to seize Jesus in the

Garden of Gethsemane, one of his followers strikes off the ear of the servant of the high priest. John adds that it was Peter who committed the act and that the servant's name was Malchus, while Luke reports that Jesus restored the ear. John also reports that, when Jesus was subsequently brought before the high priest to be questioned, one of the men who brought him slapped him; though the gospel does not say so, many readers have assumed that this was done (ungratefully, if so) by Malchus. It does not say in the gospels that any punishment was visited upon the man who struck Jesus, but a legend to that effect seems to have been current in the 6th century, when the *Leimonarium of Eucrates* told the story of a repentant heretic brought to tears after meeting a wretched Ethiopian who claimed to be the man who struck Jesus, still suffering the consequences of his unbelief.

That the 13th century legend of the Wandering Jew is a descendant of this tale seems likely; the tale crops up three times in the 13th century in different places and different versions, which have approximately as much in common with one another as they have with the *Leimonarium*'s account of the accursed Ethiopian. The name and nationality of the Wanderer have been altered, but the underlying message remains much the same: here is a living man who can testify to the actual existence and real miraculous power of Christ, and the foolhardiness of setting oneself against Him. The first surviving record of the legend as we know it dates from 1223 and appears in a Latin chronicle from Bologna; it tells of a Jew encountered by pilgrims in Armenia, who had taunted Jesus as he was going to his martyrdom and was told "I shall go, but you will await me until I come again." Ever since, the said Jew had been rejuvenated to the apparent age of 30 at hundred-year intervals.

In referring to waiting rather than moving–thus echoing the passage from John–this version stresses the immortality of the Jew rather than his restlessness, an emphasis that was to cause many later writers to wonder whether his punishment was really so terrible. This doubt was re-emphasized five years later by a more extensive account of this same story, which was much more widely copied and read. This was first recorded by the English monk Roger of Wendover, who was one of a sequence of writers working at the Benedictine monastery at St. Albans on a history of the world begun by John de Cella.

Roger claims that St. Albans had been recently visited by an Armenian archbishop, who was questioned on the subject of rumors about an immortal man (nothing is said here about his being a Jew) named Joseph. The archbishop replied that he had actually met the man in question, who had been a hall-porter in the service of Pontius Pilate, named Cartaphilus. This Cartaphilus had slapped Jesus on the back as he was being removed to be crucified, urging him to move faster, whereupon the fateful words–again referring to waiting rather than walking–were spoken to him. The report further adds that Cartaphilus was later baptized by the same man who baptized St. Paul, and had become a penitent ascetic, now very ardent in the service of the Lord. The archbishop seems to have told the same story elsewhere, because it also crops up in a poem penned by Philippe Mouskes, the archbishop of Tournai, in 1243.

Roger of Wendover's account was reproduced, initially without any substantial changes, by his successor as chronicler at St. Albans, Matthew Paris, who extended the chronicle to the year 1259 (in which year he presumably died). In later versions of the chronicle, Matthew supplemented the story with endorsements by other supposed witnesses who had visited or come from Armenia. Various version of the St. Albans chronicle were copied and distributed abroad, Matthew Paris's ultimate version being widely circulated and translated. In some of the later versions, the name used is not Cartaphilus but Buttadeus, which seems to be a bad Latinist's rendering of "God-striker." Its distribution was, however, subject to the limitations of the manuscript medium; the next important stage in the popularization of the legend came, inevitably, after the advent of printing–a technology whose destruction of the Church's virtual monopoly on the reproduction of ideas became part and parcel of the Reformation and the subsequent wars of religion.

The St. Albans chronicle was translated into German for a printed version in the 1580s; not long afterwards, in 1602–at a time when the plague was running riot in parts of Germany–a pamphlet printed in German appeared entitled *Kurtze Beschreibung von einem Juden mit Namen Ahasverus*. This was 15 years after the pamphlet that popularized the legend of Faust; both items were elements of an angst-ridden flood of popular Millenarian literature anticipating an imminent Apocalypse. The story the pamphlet tells is attributed (apocryphally, one presumes) to Paul von Eitzen, Bishop of Schleswig, who had died in 1598. The bishop is said to have encountered "a very tall person" in a church in Hamburg in 1542, and to have learned from him that his name was Ahasuerus. This Ahasuerus had been a shoemaker in Jerusalem and had cried out in anger when Jesus, carrying his cross, had stopped for a moment to rest against

27

the wall of his house–whereupon Jesus replied: "I will stand here and rest, but you must walk." After this, Ahasuerus was compelled to follow Jesus and witness his execution, and then to leave Jerusalem and wander about the world unceasingly, miserably but reverently certain of the truth of Christ's power and teaching. The pamphlet adds that Ahasuerus was seen in Danzig–probably the city where the text originated–as recently as the year 1599.

(The new name attached to the accursed immortal here was borrowed from the Vulgate translation of the Old Testament Book of Esther, where it is attached to the Persian emperor usually known as Xerxes; the story of Esther, in which an attempt to set up a massacre of the Jews is thwarted, is commemorated yearly at the festival of Purim, whose ceremonies had mistakenly led gentiles to associate the name Ahasuerus with Judaism.)

The contents of this German pamphlet were to be widely reprinted in new editions, translations and para-phrases; they were almost certainly re-appropriated into oral tradition, where they were sometimes amalgamated with other items of folklore. The story was eventually exported to all of the major European languages; while it was told and retold, it was presumably continually bol-stered–after the manner of modern urban folk tales–with news of more recent and local sightings of the Immortal Wanderer. Such embellishments helped to maintain the immediacy of the tale, and each new addition contrib-uted more apparent substance to the weight of hearsay evidence.

The 1602 pamphlet is as near to a "definitive" ver-sion of the story of the Wandering Jew as there is; it is the basis of most subsequent recyclings and transfigura-tions. It shifts the emphasis to walking rather than waiting, and it establishes other items of the legend that Paul Féval was to employ. The route by which the story arrived in Féval's text was, however, a long and slightly tortuous one, and by the time he turned his attention to it the basic story had undergone a remarkable proliferation. Not only had there been a flood of new fictional versions, but scholarly commentaries had begun to accumulate. Many of these concerned themselves mainly with the question of whether or not the legend had any truth in it (most thought not) but others interested themselves in two questions fundamental to Féval's elaboration of the legend: the issue of how many Wandering Jews there were, and the possible symbolic significance of the tale.

Scholars interested in the former issue were primarily concerned with the question of whether Cartaphilus and Ahasuerus were two different Wanderers–a question extensively discussed in a pamphlet published in Amsterdam in 1647, attributed to Abraham von Franckenberg. A German broadside of 1750 makes the crucial distinction that while Ahasuerus is condemned to wander, Cartaphilus is only condemned to wait–a distinction echoed by Féval. Other commentators were not content with only two accursed Immortals; Jacques Basnage's *Histoire des Juifs* (*History of the Jews*) (1706-07) reintroduced the Quranic Al-Sameri. (It is interesting to note that although Féval's elaborated cast of wanderers does not include Al-Sameri, it does include characters named in the Old Testament as having been cursed by Moses in like fashion.)

The symbolic significance of the Accursed Wanderer was extensively discussed by Johann Jacob Schudt's *Jüdische Merckwürdigkeiten* (1714-18), which concludes that Ahasuerus ought not to be imagined as a single person at all, but as the entire Jewish people. Schudt's was an influential work insofar as future scholarship was concerned; its thesis was reiterated by J. G. Heinsius and Carl Anton. The latter's pamphlet added nothing to the legend or the debate in itself, but Anderson points out that it provoked a scathing reply from Maria Krüger, the wife of one of Anton's colleges at the University of Helmstedt, who stoutly defended the actuality of the Accursed Wanderer. In an expanded version of her original pamphlet, Krüger added a fanciful account of her own encounters, not merely with the Wandering Jew but with a Wandering Jewess who accompanied him.

Many earlier accounts of Ahasuerus had credited him with being a married man–a common version of his story had him hold up his infant son to watch Christ go by on his way to crucifixion–but most had assumed that the curse had robbed him of her company and forced him to outlive all his family members by a vast margin; Krüger's claim suggests otherwise. Anderson claims that Krüger's pamphlet remained unknown and uninfluential, but concedes the remarkableness of the coincidence that this notion, first raised in an overt reply to a scholarly treatise insisting upon the symbolic nature of the Wandering Jew, was subsequently integrated into literary works that made much of that symbolism, further enhancing it by making the Wandering Jewess equally symbolic. The works in question, by Edgar Quinet and Eugène Sue, were key precursors of Féval's novella.

- *The Literature of the Wandering Jew in France:*

The tale of the Accursed Jew began to receive considerable attention in France in the years following the publication of the crucial German pamphlet, which was translated into French in 1605. Significantly, it is the French translation, *Discours Véritable d'un Juif Errant*, (*True Story of the Wandering Jew*) that gave the character his modern name; German references to *Der Ewige Jude* (The Eternal Jew) had continued to stress his immortality rather than his restlessness, despite the substitution of walking for waiting within the body of the tale. A 1609 version of the French *Discours* had a *complainte*–a lyric lament–attached to it, in which the Wanderer makes much of the quality of his suffering, emphasizing that immortality is no boon in combination with eternal restlessness.

French attitudes to the story were initially dismissive, as they have always tended to be of manifest foreign imports. The Parisian lawyer Raoul Boutrays (who Latinized his signature as Boterius) referred to it in a condescending manner in 1610, as did a French Jesuit named Julius Boulenger, also writing in Latin. It did not take long, however, for domestic versions of the tale to appear, with its German origins de-emphasized. One that has survived is an anonymous chapbook published in 1650 or thereabouts, entitled *Histoire Admirable du Juif Errant* (*Admirable Story of the Wandering Jew*); this appears to have been the principal source of most subsequent French literature featuring the character.

The story of the crucial encounter with the Wandering Jew, still located in Hamburg, is only the first of this version's five chapters. The second tells of his birth, but the third and fourth are inspirational accounts of episodes in the career of Jesus–the first of them dealing with the Three Kings and the flight into Egypt, the second with Jesus' preaching in the Temple–while the fifth fuses an account of the Crucifixion and the Jew's pun-

ishment with a life of Judas. Alongside this untidy elaboration–whose nature and structure are echoed by Dumas
in *Isaac Laquedem*–the lyric lament appended to the
1609 *Discours* appears to have taken on a life of its own.
It crops up subsequently in numerous variants traced by
Anderson, including some specialist Breton forms in
which it was fused with items of local folklore.

Anderson pays particular attention to the Breton
versions of the tale, both in ballads and tales seemingly
current before 1600–eight of the ten French folk tales he
tabulates are from that region–but they are primarily remarkable with respect to Féval's use of the story in that
he does not appear to have been aware of any of them.
Given that Féval took such pride in his novels about the
history of Brittany, and made such lavish use of Breton
folklore in his short stories, this is a trifle surprising; it
serves to emphasize the fact that the Breton folklore with
which he was familiar was not necessarily ancient, and
may have retained only slender connections with tales
and ballads current in the 16th century.

Anderson quotes extensively from the *complainte*
attached to the 1609 *Discours*, which is mostly formed
in pentameters, but observes that simpler verses began to
circulate later in the century. By far the most important
item in this tradition, however, appeared towards the end
of the 18th century, relating to an alleged sighting of
Ahasuerus in Brussels on April 22, 1774. This is celebrated in a Belgian *complainte* that came to be known as
the Brabantine ballad, which was spread far and wide
throughout France by means of an "Image d'Epinal," a
pictorial print illustrating the Jew's confrontation with
the burghers of Brussels, beneath which were reproduced the 24 stanzas of the ballad. This became so well-
known as an item of popular culture that the first edition

of Larousse (1766-76) took the trouble to reproduce the ballad in full. Féval had not had the opportunity to read Larousse when he wrote his novella, but he must have seen a copy of the print, which he places in the possession of the nurse Fanchon, a keen collector of Images d'Epinal. It is the opening lines of this ballad that the unfortunate Fanchon begins to sing in Chapter X of *The Wandering Jew's Daughter*, and it is the final verse that completes Féval's story.

The Brabantine ballad stimulated many imitations in France, its most important derivative being an 1831 lyric by the French poet Pierre de Béranger (1780-1857), which was intended to be sung to a familiar tune, although new music was eventually provided for it by Charles Gounod. Béranger's poem was given a dramatic new lease of life in 1856, when the famous illustrator Gustave Doré set out to produce a series of engravings based on it. (Doré, always keen to avoid overmuch limitation by the texts he illustrated, had Béranger's original bulked out by several further verses added by Pierre Dupont.) This illustrated edition of the augmented poem was reprinted in 1860, and might have been the immediate inspiration of Féval's story; it too was reckoned sufficiently important as a cultural artifact to have its own entry in Larousse.

Although the Brabantine ballad was by no means the only work inspired by the 1609 *complainte*, it was by far the most important, and it was probably known to all the later writers who used the motif, including the Polish count Jan Potocki, who gave the Wandering Jew a walk-on part in the early chapters of *Le Manuscrit Trouvé à Saragosse* (tr. as *The Saragossa Manuscript*), allegedly first published in 1804.

In between the first appearance of the Brabantine ballad and Doré's pictorial interpretation of Béranger, the literary career of the Wandering Jew had taken vast strides in France, becoming even more feverishly restless. Anderson attributes the late 18th century and early 19th century transfiguration of the Wandering Jew to the Romantic movements that spread from Germany to France and England in that era, particularly their Gothic extensions; he is undoubtedly correct to do so, but is important to note that the temper of French Romanticism was somewhat distinctive, far less attracted to Gothic horror than its German and English counterparts. For this reason, the development of the Wandering Jew as a literary character began in an idiosyncratic vein, and was extrapolated to a uniquely wondrous extreme.

Although the earliest significant French Romantic works featuring the Wandering Jew were theatrical melodramas, they were soon overshadowed by the uses of the legend made by Edgar Quinet (1803-1875), the author of *Les Tablettes du Juif-Errant* (*The Tablets of the Wandering Jew*) (1823) and the much more celebrated *Ahasvérus* (1833). The former uses its central character as a witness to a sequence of scenes from history designed–like Voltaire's *Candide* before it–to demonstrate the folly of the Leibnizian assertion that ours is the best of all possible worlds. Quinet's account of the history of religion, and the Catholic Church in particular, is a deeply skeptical one, although he is respectful of a fundamental religious impulse.

Ahasvérus is a much weightier work: an epic verse drama in four acts, which echoes the chronicle of St. Albans in venturing to present an entire history of the world, with a frame narrative set in 3,000 years after the Day of Judgment. Following the prologue, the first act offers an account of the creation and early history of the Earth–much of it narrated by a sphinx–leading to the birth of Christ. The second introduces its protagonist, here equipped with an immortal horse, and extends to the fall of the Roman Empire. The third act, set in the Middle Ages, describes an Earth allegedly in decay and dying. Here, the Wandering Jew is joined by an angel named Rachel, who has taken pity on him and has been expelled from Heaven in consequence–a character seemingly divided in Féval's story into the Wanderer's daughter, Ruthael, and the angel that continually urges him on.

Quinet's Rachel, by contrast, falls in love with the Wandering Jew (known to her as Joseph) and marries him. The marriage is followed, bizarrely, by a witches' sabbath in Strasbourg Cathedral. The fourth act casually overleaps recent history to move into the future, offering an account of the apocalypse strikingly different to the Revelation of St. John, which ends with a resolution in which Ahasuerus faces judgment on behalf of all humankind, whose symbol he has become–with Christ as his redeemer. In the epilogue that concludes the frame narrative, however, God dies in His turn and His Creation is swallowed by the vast abyss of cosmic time.

Quinet's symbolic Wandering Jew was like none that had gone before, and bears little enough resemblance to any that were to come after him, but he was the obvious inspiration–in strikingly different ways–of both Eugène Sue's symbolic Ahasuerus and Alexandre Dumas' far-ranging Isaac Laquedem. Despite the fact that Féval and Quinet had nothing in common philosophically, Quinet's Ahasuerus echoes just as resonantly in Féval, in yet another distinctive fashion. It is possible that Féval took the notion of Ahasuerus having a female companion direct from Quinet, but there is yet another version of the story, with which he was undoubtedly familiar, that may have given him a nudge in that direction.

Alongside the serial version of Dumas' *Isaac Laquedem*, an opera called *Le Juif Errant* (The Wandering Jew) was premièred in Paris, on April 23, 1852. The music was by Fromental Halévy, the words by Eugène Scribe and Jules-Henri Vernoy de Saint-Georges. Ahasuerus does not have a female companion in this version of the story, but it does begin with his confiding of a child (Irène, the grand-daughter of the assassinated Comtesse de Flandre) to the care of the heroine, a ferrywoman named Theodora. The plot then moves to Constantinople, but the opera ends with Ahasuerus–in spite of all his heroic labors in the course of the plot–being commanded to be on his way by an angel, because he is still required to witness the Last Judgment. The fact that this latter motif echoes so resonantly in Féval's story probably implies that the opening situation was similarly suggested by the opera.

There is a further work by Edgar Quinet that requires mention, because it was crucial to the uses made of Ahasuerus by Sue and Féval, even though it has nothing to do with the Wandering Jew. Quinet was a historian as well as a poet, and he was a close friend of Jules Michelet (1798-1874), the greatest of the Romantic historians and a significant modern champion of "narrative"–as opposed to disinterestedly factual–history; it was once said of him that no other historian ever cared less for accuracy. Michelet was an enthusiastic supporter of Louis-Philippe in the July Revolution of 1830, but he later became a critic of the new regime. He was dismissed from his post as professor at the Collège de

France and keeper of the National Archives following Louis-Napoleon's *coup d'état* and (like so many of the characters in this narrative history) was sent into exile. Quinet was also appointed a professor at the Collège in 1842, when he immediately began a collaboration with Michelet on a stridently anti-clerical study, *Les Jésuites* (*The Jesuits*) (1843). This was undoubtedly the book that inspired Sue to make the Jesuits the villains of his version of *The Wandering Jew*, which began serialization the following year. Even at the height of his supposed dissipation, it was a book of which Féval must have disapproved very strongly, and following the "conversion" that caused him to reissue a slightly hyped-up version of *The Wandering Jew's Daughter* he wrote a counterblast to it in his own *Jésuites* (*Jesuits*) (1877)!

Although Féval does not even deign to mention Quinet or Sue in his novella, they are clearly present in spirit, not so much as enemies to be overcome as heretics in need of correction. It is thanks to their exotic ventures–with a little help from Scribe, Vernoy de Saint-Georges, Dumas and Doré–that Féval was so strongly seized by the notion that there was not merely one itinerant Immortal but a host of them, including one loyal companion and a confused crowd of enemies. It is also thanks to them, and his perceived need to contradict them, that Féval's Ahasuerus/Laquedem becomes symbolic of a set of religious and political values very different from theirs, opposed neither to Kings nor to Jesuits, and painstakingly intolerant of opposition to either.

(It may be worth noting here that the usually-reliable Anderson gives a slightly misleading description of *The Wandering Jew's Daughter*, incorrectly suggesting that because Féval's Ahasuerus is a "supporter of liberty," he intervenes on the side of Louis-Philippe's supporters during the July Revolution. As readers of this translation will see, his sympathies tend in the opposite direction, although his actions are scrupulously even-handed in offering succor to all. Anderson also says that "of actual satire there is very little," although the reader may well feel that, given the total length of the work, the proportion of satire within it is far from "very little.")

* *The Multiplicity of Wandering Jews:*

As has already been noted, the multiplication of Wandering Jews began when scholars began to try to sort out the accumulating mass of legends and folk tales, although the Bible offered other candidates that were assimilable to the package. There is, however, another factor that helped increase the potential number of characters associated with the legend. Another consequence of its rapid spread in the age of printing was a rash of impostors who actually claimed to be the Wandering Jew.

Anderson lists 29 such impostors, carefully dividing them up into "real" and "fictitious" impostors, on the grounds that some of them are likely to be fakes twice over. (He includes the Brussels visitation as an unreliable account of an alleged impostor.) Sabine Baring-Gould, in his own pioneering essay on the legend–the first item in his notable survey of *Curious Myths of the Middle Ages* (1866)–offers accounts of three 19th century impostors recorded in England, but is content to remain undecided as to whether these men were charlatans or "unhappy lunatics" who actually believed themselves to be the Wandering Jew, as Féval's Doctor Lunat is alleged to have done.

The proliferation of such impostors undoubtedly helped to encourage Féval to imagine a whole population of both real and imaginary Wandering Jews. Herodias, he appropriated from Sue, and others he took straight from the pages of the Old Testament, but his chief counterpart to Ahasuerus–the arch-villain Ozer–has a more interesting and convoluted history.

Giovanni Marana, a native of Genoa who was resident in Paris in the late 17th century, published in 1684 what he alleged to be a translation of a work he had earlier written in Italian, entitled *L'Espion du Grand-Seigneur et Ses Relations Secrètes Envoyées au Divan de Constantinople* (tr. 1686 as *Letters Writ by a Turkish Spy, Who Lived Five and Forty Years Undiscover'd at Paris*). It is doubtful that Marana actually was a Turkish Spy, and he is probably an early contributor to the rich French tradition of fake memoirs that was carried into the 19th century by Etienne-Léon Lamothe-Langon, as well as to the tradition of salacious tales that burst into much fuller flower in the 18th. His account of a visit from the Wandering Jew is likely to be entirely fictitious rather than a record of an impostor, but it did add considerably to the legend, as well as demonstrating its literary potential more clearly than most of the versions that had gone before.

Marana's supposed visitor claimed to be called Michob Ader and to have been an officer in the Court where Jesus was condemned. The consequent account of what this Michob Ader said uses the familiar story as a launching pad for opinionated observations on the careers of such famous historical persons as Nero, Saladin, Suleiman the Magnificent and Tamerlane. He is obviously the source of the character Féval calls Ozer, but the route he followed in arriving in Féval's text is a trifle tortured.

Given that Féval makes no reference to any authentic source, except Matthew Paris, he was obviously unfamiliar with Marana's book and with the first French novel to make further use of it, Simon Tyssot de Patot's *Voyages et Aventures de Jacques Massé* (*Voyages and Adventures of Jacques Massé*) (1710), whose Wandering Jew introduces himself as Michob. He might well have been familiar with a subsequent book whose brief account of the Wandering Jew is primarily based on Marana's, Dom Augustin Calmet's *Dictionnaire de la Bible* (*Dictionary of the Bible*) (722)–Calmet's 1746 discourse on the vampires of Hungary and its neighboring regions seems to have been the inspiration of the vampire legends he made up for the purposes of *La Vampire* (1856; tr. and published by Black Coat Press as *The Vampire Countess*) and *Vampire City*–but if he consulted that work directly, he took little enough from it, although it may be worth observing that under "Ader"–in a different context–Calmet gives the alternative spelling "Oder." Because Calmet's *Dictionnaire* was a standard source for French scholars, however, it had probably helped Michob Ader and the Brabantine ballad's Ahasuerus to maintain parallel "careers" as tacit rivals long before Féval elected to exaggerate the rivalry to the level of mortal enmity. At any rate, Calmet's *Dictionnaire*, or a dim memory of it, probably helped Marana's Michob Ader to became Féval's body-stealing Ozer–a far nastier but also far more enterprising and interesting individual.

Having said all this, it seems probable that the chief motive for Féval's reckless multiplication of Wandering Jews was neither the prompting of scholars and impostors, nor the desire to provide his heroic Ahasuerus with

a villainous counterpart, but was simply his acknow-
ledgement of what had gone before in the literary arena.
The chief multipliers of Wandering Jews, in his eyes,
must have been Béranger, Quinet, Sue, Scribe and Vernoy de Saint-Georges, Dumas and Doré–and it was also
those manipulators of the legend that provided the back-
cloth to his own symbolic schema. Féval's schema is, of
course, an absurd one, whose frank preposterousness
serves to ridicule the earnest aspirations of those that had
gone before–but its farcicality does not prevent it having
a moral depth and force of its own. As with many wry
farceurs, Féval is at his most serious when he is least
earnest, and when he presents his crowd of Christ-
mockers as a ludicrous rabble, it is to emphasize his ac-
cusation, not to soften it. *The Wandering Jew's Daughter* is not a *roman à clef*, so there is probably no point in
looking for specific equivalents between the individual
tenants of Féval's House of Jews (not all of whom are
actually Jews) and the writers to whose Wandering Jews
he was objecting, but a vague general equivalence is
certainly implicit.

Here, then, is Féval's calculatedly hasty and breez-
ily impatient reply to his peers, and his account of his
own frustration in the face of what he considered to be
their unreasonably stubborn apostasy.

The Wandering Jew's Daughter

I. Vicomte Paul's Household

Paul could not be taken to the grand dinner at the Prefecture, although he was a Vicomte and most certainly the most important person in the house. He was not invited to the grand dinner, nor to the grand ball that would follow the grand dinner. The truth was that Paul did not yet belong to that category of overgrown children who dine and dance at the Prefecture.

Vicomte Paul was just coming up to 11 years old. He was a fine lad, cheerful and proud, who looked you straight in the face with his large, deep blue eyes, as tumultuous as they were caressing. He was tall for his age, lithe and graceful. He mounted his Little-Grey–the prettiest pony in Touraine–with a superior air. His tutor, Abbé Romorantin, had taught him to spell, but not well, and Joli-Coeur, the old hussar, had showed him how to draw a sword. Paul was already talking about killing all the Englishmen in England, although the English had done nothing to him; as yet, he did not know Sir Arthur.

Who is Sir Arthur?

Be patient!

Paul wanted to kill all Englishmen because he was French. Joli-Coeur admitted the solidity of that argument. Joli-Coeur detested Englishmen himself, because they were English, born in England and speaking French very badly.

Monsieur Galapian, who managed the business affairs of Vicomte Paul's father, the Colonel Comte de Savray, was scornful of Joli-Coeur's political opinions. He said that England was the foremost among nations, offering to the world, as he put it, "a fine example of a free people."

That remarkable phrase is endlessly repeated in all newspapers that sell 400,000 copies–and for a newspaper to sell 400,000 copies, it has to feature such remarkable phrases. But Vicomte Paul replied to the phrase: "Shut up, Monsieur Addition. The English put their poor folk in prison and flog their soldiers!" You will appreciate that there was something of Joli-Coeur in that.

Vicomte Paul called Monsieur Galapian "Monsieur Addition" because this man of business who dealt with the English tried in vain to teach him Monsieur Bezout's arithmetic,[1] as approved by the University.

Madame Honoré, or more simply Fanchon, a good soul from Lamballe in Brittany, was also part of Vicomte Paul's household, in the capacity of nurse. "Nurse" was merely a title. Louise de Louvigné, Comtesse of Savray, had accepted all the duties of maternity, having had all the joys. Vicomte Paul, fortunate child, had never sucked at any breast but his mother's–but Fanchon had rocked him to sleep. Fanchon loved him dearly and spoiled him as she pleased. Fanchon knew hundreds of sad songs–and besides, Fanchon was the only one in that house full of ancestral portraits who had one-*sou* prints [2] prettier than the precious canvases. That, at least, was Vicomte Paul's opinion.

In addition to Fanchon, there was also the little monkey-like groom Sapajou and Lotte, Comtesse

---

[1] See Notes page 224.

Louise's ward. The latter was a lovely creature, sad and sweet, but she was known as *the Wandering Jew's daughter*–though not in front of the masters.

Why was Lotte called *the Wandering Jew's daughter*? And why not in front of everyone?

II. Vicomte Paul's Parents

So, Vicomte Paul's dear mother was named Louise. She was the god-daughter of King Louis XVIII. Vicomte Paul's dear father, Colonel Comte Roland de Savray, was in command of the Third Hussars, garrisoned at Tours. He was 35 years old; his wife was 26. They were both handsome and good; they spent a princely fortune in an aristocratic manner.

It was said in the town–for happy people are surrounded by jealousy–that on the eve of their marriage, Monsieur de Savray had been a cavalry sub-lieutenant without a penny, though richly indebted, and a great one for playing baccarat.

It was also alleged that, although she was the King's god-daughter, Louise's fortune was more brilliant than solid. No one knew where her tenant farmers lived. The gossips who are always whispering about bad omens even said that little Vicomte Paul, brought up like a prince, could well be brought down a peg one fine day.

Singularly, the name of Lotte was often mixed up in these prognostications of envious desire. Why? We cannot tell.

What we can say, straight away, is that Lotte did not wish ill-fortune upon anyone, and that she was in the household by virtue of charity.

III. How the Comte and Comtesse Were Once Disobeyed by Their Only Son

Vicomte Paul was not invited to the Prefecture; it had been necessary to leave him behind in the house. This was no small matter. Vicomte Paul did not like others to enjoy themselves without him, and he was, to some extent, the sovereign master in the opulent villa that had been leased expressly for him, which overlooked from the height of its florid terraces the broad river, the town and the vast forests beyond: the whole of the beautiful Tourainean landscape. The air here was better for Vicomte Paul.

It is always necessary that tyrants be brought down. The Corybants sang and danced on the isle of Crete to prevent Saturn from hearing the cries of the infant Jupiter.[3] When the harnessed carriage came to the foot of the steps to await Colonel de Savray and the beautiful Comtesse Louise, in order to take them to the Prefecture–he in his dress uniform, she in a new summer outfit–the entire household took hold of Vicomte Paul, singing and dancing like Corybant priests.

They did this work so well that Comte Roland and Comtesse Louise, laughing like two mischievous schoolchildren playing truant, were able to go down the hill and take the main road to Tours at the gallop, without incurring the veto of their lord and master, that superb urchin, Vicomte Paul.

It is true that Louise was very remorseful that she had not given him a hug before departure. For the entire length of the journey, they talked about him, and the young mother's smile was dampened more than once. The child was idolized.

When Monsieur le Comte and Madame la Comtesse went into the Prefecture, there was a considerable stir. The excited Prefect dispensed several smiles and went so far as to ask for news of Vicomte Paul–yes, even the Prefect!

Among the ladies and gentlemen awaiting the soup, the conversation went along the following lines:

"A Colonel at 35!" the President said, with eulogistic bitterness. "That's what they call some going."

"A General soon," added the Municipal Treasurer's wife, an enthusiast.

"Seems a little too pleased with himself," said the Municipal Treasurer, "and his influence."

"He's got plenty to be pleased about," the Mayor observed.

"Two hundred thousand a year," the Municipal Treasurer calculated.

"His wife's credit..." the Brigade Commander's wife began, sharply.

"Always well turned-out, his wife," exclaimed the Treasurer's wife.

"God-daughter of the King!" Monsieur Lamadou, the Commandant of the Gendarmerie, put in.

"There's a story going round..." the Treasurer's wife insinuated.

"More than one!" the Brigade Commander's wife put in. *The one about the Wandering Jew's a funny one!*"

"And that dazzling Colonel likes his card-games, you know," said the Public Prosecutor.

"They might easily come a cropper," several voices sang in chorus.

The doors opened, giving passage to the happy words:

"Dinner is served, Madame!"

Sir Arthur had said nothing at all.

IV. Who Sir Arthur Was

He was a fair-haired Englishman who probably came from England. He dispensed a good deal of money, but few words. He played for high stakes with the Colonel and danced with Countess Louise.

In those days, Tours in Touraine was host to a great poet who wrote advertising slogans for confectionery and chocolate. This was the night that inspiration visited him. Now, this poet lived in an attic directly opposite Sir Arthur's house, and this poet reported that every night, at midnight, Sir Arthur wept and wailed on a balcony, saying: "I'm choking! I'm dying! Take this Galilean and his cross away from me!"

Poets are not renowned for the solidity of their heads.

But we would do better, instead of reporting these stupidities, to confess frankly that we have not the slightest idea who Sir Arthur was.

V. Vicomte Paul's Plan of Campaign

Vicomte Paul would not have been deceived if he had not had important matters to attend to that day. Vicomte Paul was French; he loved his country. Without being scornful of the diversions appropriate to his age, he was acquainted with serious matters.

The main road from Paris to Tours extended as far as Nantes, and even to Saint-Nazaire. The events of our story occurred during the Restoration; railways did not yet exist. Given that the highway extended as far as Saint-Nazaire, a little port fully exposed to English enterprise, Paul had wondered how the capital might be shielded from a surprise attack.

I suppose the English, dressed in red swallow-tailed coats and commanded by Wellington, having disembarked at Saint-Nazaire, might take Paimbeuf, conquer Nantes, storm Ancenis, Angers, Bourgueuil, Langenis and Luynes... You shrug your shoulders? In the time of Charles VI, and even more recently, the English have taken plenty of others!

Anyway, let's not quarrel. This much is true: at the end of the garden, there was a pavilion that overlooked the Loire and the road: an excellent position to prevent Wellington from passing through. Vicomte Paul, assisted by Joli-Coeur and four gardeners, was in the process of raising formidable defenses around this pavilion. The Colonel had given permission to divert water from the reservoir to fill the moats; Comtesse Louise had promised a cannon.

I beg you to consider Wellington and his English forces, all decorated with red coat-tails, emerging from Luynes to the tune of *Marlborough's Going to War* and marching on Paris. They would not expect to find Vicomte Paul's fortifications there! Bang bang! Boom boom! Musket-fire! Cannon-fire! See how they flee, showing off their funny backs!

Shall they escape? Certainly not! Vicomte Paul throws himself on to his pony, catches up with Wellington, seizes him by his coat-tails and avenges the martyrdom of Joan of Arc! And then, on to Tours, singing the *Te Deum*, to dine at the Prefecture. This time, Vicomte Paul would be invited, I think! He would certainly have deserved it.

VI. In Which Vicomte Paul Shows Himself to be a Fine Prince

Today, Joli-Coeur did this work with an unaccustomed vigor. The Comte and Comtesse had given him the word. The four gardeners plied their picks and wheeled their barrows to marvelous effect. It was a matter of putting up a wall, whose sole purpose would be to make Wellington shiver and to put any idea of attacking Vicomte Paul's fortress out of his head.

Vicomte Paul had his Commandant-General's telescope and inspected the road to see whether the English, forewarned by clever spies, had redoubled their efforts in order to catch him off guard before the work was completed.

Suddenly, Vicomte Paul let out a cry of surprise and his handsome brow became furrowed.

"Is it Wellington?" asked Joli-Coeur.

"The calèche!" the Vicomte replied, reddening with anger. "The new one! La Brie on the bench, Landerneau and Lafleur behind, all three in full livery and freshly powdered. I've been betrayed! Mama and Papa are going to dine in town!"

The four gardeners stopped work in consternation. Joli-Coeur scratched his ear.

"My horse!" cried the child. "I'll catch up with them."

"Little-Grey's having the shoes on his forehooves replaced," Joli-Coeur replied, touching his head to his forelock as if he were saluting his officer.

"Then, I'll take Papa's horse. Let's see! Do as I say!"

The four gardeners shook their heads—and I don't know what Joli-Coeur did—while the side-door of the calèche, which was turning a corner, displayed blonde hair studded with precious stones that sparkled in the sunlight and a translucent handkerchief waving.

"Dear mother!" cried Vicomte Paul, holding out his arms. "If you had asked my permission, I would have told you to go, I assure you! Dear father—you, of all people, should not display fear!"

He was weeping, but he was laughing, blowing kisses and saying:

"Does mother look beautiful? I would have liked to see Papa with his medals! Go on, wretches, enjoy yourselves. Eat ice cream! Dance! Me, I'll guard the house."

VII. Vicomte Paul's Idea

Having said this, while stifling a noble sigh, Vicomte Paul sent his blessing to the calèche as it disappeared behind the poplars.

"To work!" he commanded.

The pickaxes pecked away, the wheelbarrows rolled more lustily. The work went on in this fashion for three minutes. Then, Vicomte Paul had a good idea, which he formulated thus:

"I shall have the Prefecture Dinner in the house! I shall be Papa; Lotte shall be Mama. Monsieur Galapian shall be the Prefect, Abbé Romorantin shall be his wife, Fanchon will be all the ladies, and you Joli-Coeur, shall be the General. I want all the little boys and girls from the farm to dance until 6 a.m... We'll all dine here, in the pavilion. Let the English beware! We'll drink champagne and tell stories. There'll be liqueurs. You'll have permission to smoke!"

As he spoke, Vicomte Paul became more animated. As he pronounced the last words, he turned a dangerous somersault and concluded thus:

"If Mama and Papa get angry, I'll run away to sea!"

VIII. Belshazzar's Feast [4]

Believe me or not, it was a superb dinner–even better than the one at the Prefecture. Oh, much better.

The cook, having received Vicomte Paul's orders, improvised an abundant and sugary menu to accompany the usual bill of fare that was already cooking on the spit and in the cooking-pots. There were no less–and no more–than five courses. The linen tablecloth was set out in the pavilion, the terror of the English and the boulevard of France. A determined attack was mounted on the cellar, which was poorly defended by the cellarman. Bordeaux, Chambertin and champagne were all carried off. To settle the bill, the cellarman was invited to come too.

There was no negotiation. Vicomte Paul was the master. Even Abbé Romorantin gave in with good grace.

Five o'clock chimed: at the exact moment when the usher down below called out "Dinner is served, Madame!" Sapajou, in his best livery, came to announce that "the soup was on the table". He was told off, for Vicomte Paul knew how things were done in high society, but he was permitted to take his place among the farm children, arranged like pickets and redder than poppies. He promised that on future occasions he would say: "Dinner is served, Monsieur le Vicomte!"

Vicomte Paul was seated between Fanchon, who represented the ladies, and General Joli-Coeur. Fanchon had brought a thick wad of pictorial prints. Facing the Vicomte was little Lotte, between Monsieur Galapian and Abbé Romorantin.

"Take the soup away!" Vicomte Paul commanded. "This is a feast. No one can force us to eat soup."

IX. Lotte

Down at the Prefecture, the Brigade Commander's wife had said, with regard to Comte Roland de Savray and the beautiful Comtesse Louise, god-daughter of Louis XVIII:

"There's more than one story... the one about the Wandering Jew's a funny one!"

Many people might wonder what connection there was between the brilliant fortune of this young married couple and the Accursed Wanderer of popular legend.

Meanwhile, here in the pavilion, face-to-face with Vicomte Paul, there was a pretty and pale creature, as sweet as the melancholy smiles of the saints, whom the people of the house and the surrounding countryside called *the Wandering Jew's daughter*.

Lotte appeared to be eight or ten years old. She was tall for that age. Those who knew her claimed that she had always been the same. For a long time–a very long time–she had seemed to be always eight or ten years old. Some of them said: "for 11 years!"

She spoke little. Her large blue eyes were often dreamy, often prayerful. Her golden-blonde hair hung down in silky tresses upon the translucent pallor of her cheeks.

There was a sort of coldness around her, a mystery, a dread, and an enchantment.

Comtesse Louise and her son Paul were the only ones who embraced her wholeheartedly.

X. Mystery

And many things were said in low voices, in the house, in the region–even in Paris, where Colonel de Savray was highly thought of at Court. Comte Roland's youth had been "stormy," to employ the sanctioned term. As I have already said–it bears repeating–he was an unrestrained gambler. Under the Empire, when he was only a sub-lieutenant, Joli-Coeur had found him hanging from a coat-rack in his room. He had shot himself in the head twice, but only grazed himself. At Lyon, one evening, when he had lost and had not the means to pay his debts, he had thrown himself into the Rhone.

After these various exploits, it was slightly astonishing to see him enjoying such flourishing health.

One evening, at Lamballe in the Côtes-du-Nord, where he was garrisoned, he fell in love with a young woman who was very noble and very poor. This was in 1812 or thereabouts. Much fun was then made of Mademoiselle Louise de Louvigné, god-daughter of Louis de Bourbon, Comte de Mittau, whom Louis XV's infantrymen insisted on calling King Louis XVIII. In France, one should never make fun of anyone or anything, even toppled thrones or banished Kings.

Sub-lieutenant Roland de Savray asked for the hand of Louise de Louvigné and obtained it. Between the two of them, in the parlance of Lamballe, they made up a poor company.

At this point, chronologically speaking, the events of the story to which the Brigade Commander's wife had alluded in the dining room had taken place–the story of the Wandering Jew. The Brigade Commander's wife had referred to that story, in regard to Comte Roland and Comtesse Louise, as one accuses certain people of having a noose in their pocket.

Instead of telling the story of the Wandering Jew, we shall point out a singular thing. The words "Wandering Jew" were strictly prohibited in the house of the Colonel Comte de Savray. Vicomte Paul, who loved legends passionately–and knew them all, thanks to his nurse, Fanchon Honoré, who possessed the best collection of pictorial prints in Touraine–did not know the legend of the Wandering Jew. No one had ever given his friend Lotte that bizarre nickname, *the Wandering Jew's daughter*, in front of him.

And one day, when Dame Fanchon was rocking the baby Vicomte Paul to sleep, with a song that went:

> "*Is there anything on Earth*
> "*That is more amazing*
> "*Than the great misery*
> "*Of the poor...*" [5]

Well, let us simply say that Louise's bell had interrupted her at the very moment when she reached the end of the fourth line, and the young Comtesse, normally so softly-spoken, had said to her sternly:

"Madame Honoré, if you wish to remain with us, never sing that!"

XI. Of the Various Effects of Chambertin

All was going well around the table in the pavilion. It was not young wine that was being drunk. Wellington could come; there would be someone to greet him.

Abbé Romorantin talked politics with Monsieur Galapian, and they caused one another some distress in doing so, as all men who are not of the same opinion do when they talk politics. The Abbé defended the throne and the altar; Galapian wanted all that done away with. The opinions of this gallant fellow were ahead of his time; he was already liberal, according to the prevailing standards of 1848. In front of the Colonel, he expressed himself more prudently, but the Colonel was not there and Chambertin loosens the tongue.

The little Tourainean peasants were enjoying themselves wholeheartedly, all talking at once. Sapajou was recounting his family's misfortunes. Monsieur Galapian, unveiling his seditious tendencies, cried:

"Up with the charter, down with the charioteer!"[6]

Joli-Coeur talked about his campaigns; Dame Fanchon driveled on about her young days. Vicomte Paul would have given the whole house and the Prefecture, too, for Wellington to appear on the road with 100,000 Englishmen, so that he might throw bottles at their heads.

The only exception was Lotte, as cold and calm as ever; there had never been anything but pure water in her glass. Her eyelids were half-closed over the azure of her dreaming eyes. Her long hair framed the diaphanous whiteness of her cheeks with light curls.

"Sing us a song, nurse!" ordered Vicomte Paul, who wanted to experience every pleasure.

Fanchon did not have to be asked twice. She took a thick roll of laments out of her pocket and positioned her spectacles on her nose.

"Silence!" Paul commanded. "A nice one, nurse, and not one of those I know!"

As for silence, that was much called for. The Abbé, Monsieur Galapian, the little Touraineans and Joli-Coeur expressed their obedience in chorus. Nothing else could be heard!

"A nice one," Fanchon the nurse repeated. "One that you don't know. Let's see. I no longer have the eyes I had 15 years ago!" She riffled through the stack, moistening her thumb to make the decorated leaves slide more easily.

Suddenly, Vicomte Paul cried out:

"Oh, that one's lovely! I've never seen that one!"

XII. Of the Trouble Started by the Pictorial Print

Medusa, the daughter of Phorcys, displeased Minerva, the Goddess of Wisdom, who punished her by metamorphosing her hair into serpents. Thus coiffed, Medusa's head changed into stone all those who looked at her. You might say that the print–that lovely picture in gold, purple, emerald and sapphire, which cost a *sou*–produced a parallel effect among Vicomte Paul's guests.

As soon as the Vicomte's finger had drawn the attention of the guests to the picture, a sudden and profound silence fell around the table.

Lotte's gaze seemed to slip sideways and become distant beneath the silky fringe of her eyelashes, a line of white light joining her eye to the paper.

Then, her eyelids closed.

Fanchon wanted to recapture the errant leaf; she seemed to feel the consternation that weighed upon the guests more acutely than anyone else–but Vicomte Paul had already taken hold of the print and was contemplating it, saying:

"The Wandering Jew? Who is the Wandering Jew?"

At 11 years of age, had Vicomte Paul never heard talk of the Wandering Jew? We have already called attention to that singular circumstance.

There is not a six-year-old child in France who does not know the story of the Wandering Jew–and we shall soon see that at Tours, in Touraine, precisely because of Colonel de Savray and his wife, the beautiful Comtesse Louise, people were more preoccupied with the Wandering Jew than in any other region of France.

And besides, in that very château, they called that sweet child Lotte *the Wandering Jew's daughter*!

But no one had ever given her that nickname in front of Vicomte Paul.

Why not?

Remember that Comtesse Louise, in speaking of the song about the Wandering Jew, had said to his nurse, Fanchon:

"Madame Honoré, if you want to remain in with us, never sing that!"

XIII. The Print

It was a splendid September evening. The windows of the pavilion in which Vicomte Paul was imitating the great dinner at the Prefecture faced westwards, where the enlarged Sun was descending towards its bed of roseate clouds, fringed with purple and gold.

That warm light, profusely penetrating the banqueting hall, deepened the ruby redness of the wine and tinted every face with vermilion–but the print at which Vicomte Paul was pointing really was inscribed in gold, purple and flame by the ardent fire of the setting Sun. It was difficult to imagine a more marvelous print. It rippled with vivid cinnabar, the tender green of raw cabbage, shrill yellow and celestial blue. In addition to all that, it was generously embellished by the obliquely directed rays of a beaming sun. Everything in it was gold-illumined: the cornices of the Flemish houses, the feet of the table, the tresses of the women, the tips of the noses of the "ultra-civilized" burghers, and even the rags worn by the long-bearded man who was refusing the hospitality of the good people of Brussels in Brabant.

They seemed well-dressed, fat and good-humored, these burghers dressed in the manner of the times of Louis XIV. It was with evident chagrin that the bearded man drew away from the magnificent cooking-pot–decorated like everything else–and the Louvain beer crowned with golden foam.

The Brabantine women, clad like Mary Stuart, smiled down from the balconies. Swallows were flying in the sky between the pretty bell-towers of Flanders. The burgomaster's dog was between his legs, barking.

65

The women, the swallows, the bell-towers, the balustrades, the dog, the burgomaster and the calves of his legs were all illumined in gold!

Anyway, what purpose is there in describing this picture so minutely? You can buy one like it anywhere, for a sou–and there is also, into the bargain, the song printed beneath it, whose 24 couplets have been around the world a hundred times:

> *Is there anything on Earth*
> *That is more amazing*
> *Than the great misery*
> *Of the poor Wandering Jew?*
> *Whose unfortunate fate*
> *Seems sad and wearisome.*

XIV. Hush!

The worthy Abbé Romorantin was visibly disconcerted. Monsieur Galapian, a man of unprepossessing appearance, had a mocking smile upon his thick lips. The hussar Joli-Coeur scratched his ear until it bled. The little Touraineans had opened their eyes and mouths wide. Sapajou was making faces. Fanchon's head, hands and knees were all a-tremble, as if the nurse were about to faint.

The only exceptions were the faces of pretty Lotte and Vicomte Paul, each facing the other, which had not changed at all. Lotte was still cold and gentle, like the blonde angels in pious images.

Paul laughed abruptly, drew himself upright, and repeated:

"The Wandering Jew? Who is the Wandering Jew?"

No one made any response.

But when Abbé Romorantin happened to sneeze, everyone–glad to break the silence–exclaimed: "God bless you!"

The Abbé thanked them.

Vicomte Paul put his hand on his hip. "I'm going to get angry," he declared, shortly, "if no one tells me who the Wandering Jew is. I've never seen a beard like..."

Galapian sang:

> *"Never had they seen*
> *A man thus bearded..."*

"What's that you say, Monsieur Addition?" Vicomte Paul demanded.

"Hush!" hissed the business manager.

"Hush!" repeated the Abbé.

And all around the table there was a long-winded echo:

"Hush! Hush! Hush!"

XV. Vicomte Paul's Second Idea

As you might well imagine, this was not to Vicomte Paul's liking. The magnificent child was used to being obeyed. He tapped his foot and swore. Everyone was fearful, but everyone kept silent.

And to cover their confusion everyone, including Fanchon, took up their glasses of Chambertin and drank.

The Sun was slowly sinking into its dazzling bed.

"Will no one tell me," cried Vicomte Paul, "why this gentleman does not drink beer, and in what country beggars wear golden rags?"

"Madame la Comtesse has forbidden it," murmured Fanchon.

"Monsieur le Comte too," added Joli-Coeur.

"Well!" cried Vicomte Paul. "It's me who is Papa, and Lotte is Mama. We give you permission to speak– isn't that right, Lotte?"

It seemed that the oblique rays of sunlight passing over Lotte's diaphanous beauty lacked the power to color her sculpted whiteness.

"May God have pity on us!" stammered the nurse. "She was like that when I saw her for the first time..."

In a voice as sweet as a lullaby, but so faint that they did not know whether they heard her correctly, Lotte murmured:

"My father is coming..."

Vicomte Paul was not listening, because he had been struck by a new idea.

"To be sure," he said, "I'm a fool: I have only to read the legend for myself!"

XVI. A Confusion of Tongues

There was then a great tumult in the pavilion where Vicomte Paul was hosting the Prefecture dinner, while waiting for the English. Everyone got up, shouting. Monsieur Galapian was howling like the Jews one hears on the trading-floor in the Bourse; Abbé Romorantin was sneezing in distress; The little Touraineans were buzzing like flies; and Sapajou was imitating the crow of a cockerel, rather more skillfully.

Fanchon and Joli-Coeur threw themselves upon Vicomte Paul from either side, to snatch away the fatal print, which tore in two, bisecting the body of the Wandering Jew.

Lotte bowed her head and released a great sigh. That strange little girl was no longer made of alabaster; the transparency of her graceful form was increasing...

"We've drunk enough Chambertin," said the cellarman. "Shall we pass round the champagne?"

"There is no Wandering Jew!" Fanchon declared, resolutely.

"There certainly isn't!" Joli-Coeur agreed.

"It's a legendary myth," the Abbé explained.

"It's a fib," Galapian corrected him.

Sapajou also knew how to yelp like a little dog. He gave a demonstration: "Yap! Yap! Yap! Yap!"

Fanchon went on: "It's used to rock little children to sleep..."

"And to make grown-ups laugh," added Joli-Coeur.

"Even so," the Abbé objected, "there's an important Christian message underneath it."

"I don't know about that," said Joli-Coeur, "but the tune's nice."

"And easy to sing," Fanchon put in. "Listen."

She sang, in her slightly broken voice:

> *"Gentlemen, I swear to you*
> *"That I am indeed unfortunate;*
> *"Never do I pause,*
> *"Here or anywhere else;*
> *"In good weather or bad*
> *"I march incessantly..."*

"We used to say *arreste,*" the Abbé observed, "in order to preserve the rhyme.[7] That proves the antiquity of the song."

"I have good tobacco in my pipe which offers even better proof of the discovery of America!" said Galapian.

Joli-Coeur sang:

> *"Isaac Laquedem*
> *"The name given to me..."*

"Hold on," the Abbé put in. "The true name is Ahasver or Ahasuerus."

"Pardon me," Fanchon objected, "but it's definitely Isaac Laquedem..."

> *"Born in Jerusalem,*
> *"A very famous town..."*

"Matthew Paris," Galapian said, "calls him Cartaphilus."[8]

"Schedt affirms," the Abbé began, "that there was a certain Ozer, one of Herod's soldiers–the same one who extended the sponge soaked in vinegar to our Divine Savior..." [9]

"George of Trebizond claims that one named Levy..."

"Schiavone supposes..."

"El Edrisi infers..."

Meanwhile, Joli-Coeur sang, out of tune and at the top of his voice:

> *"The very sky that surrounds me*
> *"Is painful to me.*
> *"I am going round the world*
> *"For the hundredth time:*
> *"Everyone dies in his turn,*
> *"But I live forever!"*

Whereas Fanchon cooed:

> *"I have no resources*
> *"Neither home nor possessions,*
> *"I have five* sous *in my purse*
> *"That is all my worldly wealth;*
> *"In every place and time*
> *"I always have as much."*

The little Touraineans repeated the refrain, while vying to put the dessert in their pockets. The unfortunate Vicomte Paul, deafened, covered his ears and called in vain for silence.

Suddenly, however, you might have heard a pin drop.

Vicomte Paul had asked:

"But where is Lotte?"

And everyone looked at the empty seat of the one who was called *the Wandering Jew's daughter*–where they saw, in the place formerly occupied by the child, a fine cloud of vapor, completing its slow disappearance...

XVII. Sunset

Galapian and Abbé Romorantin, who had been sitting to either side of little Lotte, recoiled instinctively. The disquieted gazes of the assembled guests began to wander. Fanchon, leaning behind Vicomte Paul's chair, muttered in Joli-Coeur's ear:

"Didn't she say: *My father is coming*?"

Joli-Coeur, hussar and brave man that he was, shivered. He got up to take in some air at a window, but scarcely had he looked out over the countryside that he cried, as his legs gave way:

"Look! Look!"

"Is it the English?" asked Vicomte Paul. "Take up your weapons!"

"Lord Above!" moaned Fanchon, looking out in her turn. "Oh, Lord Above!"

The Abbé made the sign of the cross. Galapian put his pince-nez on.

The rayless Sun, a huge purple disc, was touching the line of clouds on the horizon. Violently lit from behind in this fashion, all the harmonious aspects of the land surrounding Tours, resembling an immense and flourishing garden watered by the most beautiful river in France, acquired strange tints and offered bizarre impressions. The hills grew in bulk, the distant horizons extended into fantastic profundities; night was already falling in the depths of the valleys, while the neighboring summits were illuminated with multicolored fringes.

Everyone was at the pavilion's windows, but no one was admiring this marvelous spectacle. The setting Sun could drown in these splendors; its last caress could embrace the transfigured countryside; no one was looking at the countryside or the Sun. Every eye was fixed on the same point; the same anxious astonishment was reflected in every face.

On the highest point of the road that led from Tours to Angers, a man–an apparition, rather–was visible, immediately in front of the Sun. His tall silhouette was cut out in black from the purple disc.

And the oblique light cast his enormous shadow into the very depths of the valley.

XVIII. The Traveler

At first, the man seemed to be motionless: a somber statue in the midst of dazzling light, but it was soon evident that he was moving, for his head descended from the level of the summit behind which the Sun was disappearing.

It was possible, then, to make him out more clearly. It was a man of considerable height, who supported himself as he walked with a traveler's staff.

He was alone. Or was he? As he advanced towards the shadowed valley, a white shape, indecisive and transparent, was vaguely perceptible at his side.

"Lotte!" Vicomte Paul was the first to murmur.

A muted murmur from behind replied:

"*The Wandering Jew's daughter!*"

"Now then!" muttered Monsieur Galapian, rubbing his eyes. "Have I drunk too much Chambertin?"

"*Vade retro*," stammered Abbé Romorantin.[10]

Meanwhile, the traveler arrived at the bottom of the slope and disappeared behind a curtain of poplars.

"Let's dance!" cried Vicomte Paul, astonished to find a weight upon his heart.

No one made any response.

Dame Fanchon squeezed the medallion of her rosary, trembling. Joli-Coeur drew nearer to her, murmuring:

"It was like this when he came to Lamballe... The Sun was visible in the distance, setting into the sea ."

"God preserve us from misfortune!" said the nurse.

And Vicomte Paul, shaking his blond curls in a valiant manner, cried:

"We must do here as they do at the Prefecture. Let's dance, or I'll be angry. I want everyone to dance!"

XIX. *A Corner of the Prefecture*

They were indeed dancing at the Prefecture

Prefectures are Louvres abridged, Tuileries in miniature. I once knew a Prefect who said: "My government..."

The Prefect's wife, a plump little queen, as round and red as a pony, sowed happiness among her servants by the distribution of her smiles. The garden of France is a noble country; its salons are full of beautiful girls and charming young women–but among all those admirable creatures, Comtesse Louise shone brightest of all. She was truly a queen, in spirit, generosity and beauty.

Comtesse Louise was dancing.

Those women who do not dance are suspected of being jealous of those who do–particularly those who no longer dance. I know some, however, who look with a maternal smile upon the reckless joys of youth; I know some, more numerous, who remain beautiful beneath their grey hair by virtue of benevolence and mercy. Certainly, there were dear women present here, pleasantly content to be spectators, with no regrets, and exquisite women who never grew old, at least in their hearts, and who found an eternal youth in the treasure of their charitable piety. But variety is necessary in a flower-bed, and there are always a few marigolds in the midst of roses.[11] There were also bold women who, having no charity to return, carped and slandered abundantly, and brave gentlemen who sided with these bold women.

In one corner of the salon, where the military administration, the high court, the general staff, the estates, the local treasury, and even the groves of academe, were advantageously represented, time was being killed by whatever means came to hand.

Colonel Comte Roland de Savray and Comtesse Louise were the topic of discussion.

The conversation was hushed, but biting.

"My God," said a lady of the landed gentry, "she's pretty, if one likes..."

"I, who know my poor folk," observed the Arch-Bishop, in passing, "know well enough why she has an angelic gaze!"

Out here, grandeur pays its way. Our lords the Bishops are condemned from time to time to Prefecture galas—but Monsignor was not of this company; he continued on his way.

"When one has an annual income of 100,000 *livres*," said the wife of a military Adjutant, mockingly, "one can certainly spare a few *louis* for the unfortunate, so to speak!" Never have you seen such a beautiful turban as the one she sported; she looked like Roustan, the Emperor's mameluke, although her features were more masculine.[12]

"The Colonel isn't dancing," said Monsieur Lamadou, the Commandant of the Gendarmerie.

"He's dancing with the Queen of Spades!" quipped the Public Prosecutor.

"A real card-player!" added several voices.

These Savrays were too handsome, too noble, too rich, too happy. No one in the corner liked them.

"Bah!" said the Adjutant's wife. "If he lost his wife's dowry, he'd have the Wandering Jew's five *sous*."

XX. Doctor Lunat

"It's me who's the Wandering Jew! Who's talking about my five *sous*?" said a thin, dark man with a low forehead and glittering eyes, in a soft voice.

"That dear Doctor's having one of his fits!" murmured the women.

The Commandant of the Gendarmerie, Monsieur Lamadou, said:

"He shouldn't be allowed out like this. He might break something!"

"Oh, he's perfectly harmless... nevertheless, it's that Comtesse Louise who has addled his brain!"

"Such a wise man!"

"Such a celebrated specialist!"

"What did the Comtesse de Savray do to him?" asked the Treasurer's wife, who was new to the district.

"That's right, dear," said the Adjutant's wife. "You don't know. Doctor Lunat is a remarkable alienist. He's very successful in treating madmen. He cured an old Notary who thought he was an alligator. It was very embarrassing–the Notary, I mean. He dived into his pond to catch fish. Now, thanks to Doctor Lunat, he thinks he's a fish himself, and won't go out for fear of crocodiles..."

"That's progress!" they all declared, as one.

"I certainly think so!"

"But how could the Comtesse de Savray...?" insisted Madame Direct Contributions.

"Wait a minute, and you'll understand... but look how she's enjoying herself!"

"She's a sylphide!" said the Brigade Commander, admiringly.[13]

The diamond-studded wife of the Collector of Taxes opened her pince-nez. "Rather risqué," she observed, from behind three outmoded fans.

"You'll understand, dear Madame," the military Adjutant's wife, "that Madame Lancelot, who saw the beginnings of these Savrays at Lamballe, tells a story about the Wandering Jew..."

Madame Lancelot was in Land.

The entire gallery offered this testimony: "Ah! A good story!"

"And Madame Lancelot tells it so well!"

"Well," the Adjutant's wife, continued, "this story has made the Wandering Jew fashionable, because the Savrays are not well-liked hereabouts."

"Why aren't they well-liked hereabouts?"

"I ask you! This Doctor Lunat, poor fellow, always wants to get to the bottom of all these mysteries..."

"There are mysteries, then?"

"In quantity! And Doctor Lunat, who has cured so many madmen..."

"Like the crocodile...?"

The Adjutant's wife concluded: "You see, the Comtesse de Savray is the cause of that misfortune!"

"Ladies," said Doctor Lunat, with exquisite politeness, "I cannot pause, you know, that's legendary, but I'll acquaint myself with your precious news while walking around you... besides, it's not forbidden to me to mark time." He caressed his long beard with his whole hand, even though his chin was as hairless as a little girl's.

"That could be us!" murmured the Commandant of the Gendarmerie.

Doctor Lunat seized him avidly by one of his uniform buttons.

"Don't move!" he ordered. "Look at me without squinting. I believe you're showing symptoms..."

"Will you kindly release me!" cried the peaceful soldier.

"I forbid you to move! Be still! The vulgar claim that it's necessary to have a mind to go mad. You're living proof to the contrary..."

A dozen bursts of laughter were stifled by embroidered handkerchiefs.

Doctor Lunat pirouetted on his heels and marked time energetically. "Madame," he said to the Adjutant's wife, "you are a curious specimen. At 58 years of age, you must have a few stars in your brain."

"But I'm not yet 50!" cried the Adjutant's wife, indignantly. "This madman is dangerous!"

"Colonel de Savray wins 500 *louis*," said a District Councilor.

Doctor Lunat rummaged furiously in his pocket. "I have my five *sous*!" he thought aloud, with an intimate satisfaction. "All's well! I'll be able to pay my share!"

XXI. Sir Arthur's Gaze

Comtesse Louise would not have been able to walk a kilometer, but she could dance all night without the slightest fatigue. After the quadrille, she was only a little more rosy-cheeked, and her lovely eyes were more vividly radiant.

She came into the room where her husband was playing cards; he was playing against Sir Arthur, the Englishman, who lived opposite the celebrated Touraincan poet of spicy bread.

Sir Arthur looked at Comtesse Louise in a quite indescribable fashion. It was not, however, the first time it had happened. Sir Arthur's gaze pierced the bosom of Comtesse Louise like a gimlet, and injected a kind of anguish into her heart.

"Raise you another 100 *louis*," said Colonel Comte Roland de Savray.

They were playing for high stakes that night, at the Prefecture. But then, Sir Arthur never played for petty ones.

XXII. The Wandering Jew's Five Sous

"Ladies," Doctor Lunat continued, in the ballroom, "I've been insane, there's no denying it... madder than the Public Prosecutor, who plays artificial birdsong four hours a day to teach the tune to his cat."

"That's a lie!" cried the Magistrate. "I protest! The bird belongs to my clerk's wife!"

Doctor Lunat smiled affably. "With people like that," he said, in a stage-whisper, "the best thing is to humor them. I've been insane, to the point of forgetting that I am the Wandering Jew. I had not the slightest suspicion of it. I could no longer see my beard! I thought that I was a doctor–what an astonishing thing! Let me walk a little–the angel is not pleased and is pointing a fingertip at me."

"Walk, walk!" said the Commandant of the Gendarmerie, in his deepest voice.

"Can you hear it?" said the Doctor, enigmatically. "You know that in every 100 years I'm allowed 24 hours of rest. It's not a great deal, but if I'm economical, it's sufficient. One can get used to anything. I pity settled people. Besides, rumors of the Wandering Jew are a trifle haphazard. There's truth in them, and falsehood. I can put you straight.

"The anecdote about the burghers of Brussels in Brabant is utterly apocryphal; it was in Suresnes that the Deputy Mayor and the local Constable offered me a glass of wine; I would have been able to accept it, while marking time, but I've stuck to Medoc since the early years of Louis XIII.[14] What a sly dog that Richelieu was!

"As regards my character, take the trouble to think about it for a minute. Eighteen hundred years of travel and penitence has changed me from black to white. My conduct in Jerusalem violated the most elementary principles of charity. I haven't a word to say in my defense, except that I never had any primary education. In that distant era, cobblers didn't go to the Military Academy.

"I speak lightly of this; I'm an orthodox disciple of Voltaire, but fundamentally, you understand, I know too much not to be a good Catholic. As far as philosophies go, in 1,800 years I've seen those of every shade. Here's the general formula: at the bottom of every schism, as at the bottom of every revolution, there's some bold fellow who has done something silly and is biting his fingers about it, or an imbecile who's nobody and wants to be somebody.

"Darn it, my legs are itching! Let's not talk politics. Do you know Talma? [15] I designed the costume in which he played the immemorial Augustus; I'm very fearful for my friends, you know. Eighteen hundred years of experience! And memory! I know what everyone else knows, but I also know what everyone else has forgotten: the enormous Void that has the recipe for Greek fire, with which I could make my fortune. But then, do you think that my five *sous* is nothing? I can have a vanilla ice-cream whenever I like."

Everyone listened, believe it or not.

The Doctor put an empty saucer on the tray and went on, always marching on the spot: "And, parenthetically, it was my five *sous* that brought me to my senses as the time of my crisis. Would I have had five *sous* in my pocket if I were not the Wandering Jew? When I break a 20-*sou* window, I pay in four installments–that's all there is to it. Here's a funny story: with my five farthings I made millions one day, and the Angel never caught a glimpse of it! Is that astonishing? At first impression, yes, but in the end it's as simple as saying hello. In 1822, I was traveling through Germany..."

"He has never left the country," the Leader of the Council put in.

"I made the acquaintance of a Jewish banker–an excellent fellow for a moneylender–named Schwartz. By virtue of doubling his money in every one of his deals, he finished up not having a *sou*. That's natural. He was put into fraudulent bankruptcy for the miserable sum of 500,000 francs; his situation rent my heart. I felt sorry for him. I made him buy three or four food-baskets. He gave one basket to each of his cashiers, and we left together for the countryside, me in the lead and the cashiers bringing up the rear. I had my five *sous* in my pocket. I made a hole in it and the five *sous* fell out; one of the cashiers picked them up.

"As soon as the five *sous* fell out, another five materialized, according to the Law. As the pocket still had a hole in it, they fell out like the others, and the cashier picked them up again.

"And so it went on. I can't give you any idea of the amazing rapidity with which this banking operation–one of the most ingenious of which I ever heard–proceeded.

"The five *sous* kept on falling; the cashiers ceaselessly gathered them in. As soon as one of the food-baskets was full it was emptied, its contents entrusted to the honorable farmers. It's among the inhabitants of the countryside that one still finds the fidelity of olden days. Besides, Germany is an honest country, as everyone knows; for every hundred baskets, it returned more than 36, all of them more than half-full. The cashiers didn't embezzle a *centime*, but ever since that day, they all pay their stockbrokers in cash.

"When I said a hundred baskets, that was a manner of speaking. Can you calculate how many hampers full of coppers are required to make up a sum of 500,000 francs? Personally, I haven't the slightest idea. This much is certain: we went along the Rhine in this manner from Cologne to Strasbourg–two fine cathedrals–but at the Kohl bridge, the Angel got wind of something and I was obliged to sew up my pocket.

"Do you know why everyone in Cologne is called Schwartz? The one that I saved caught a stiffness in the joints from so much bending over, and died of it. His widow wanted to marry me, but I have my own wife, Queen Herodias. She's in Paris, in the Salpêtrière, with the authorization of the Government..."[16]

XXIII. The Story

"This time," Doctor Lunat exclaimed, at this point, "the Angel's becoming annoyed. I know him; he isn't pleasant when he's angry." And he was off like a shot, stroking his non-existent beard and supporting himself with his imaginary staff.

"He cured a Notary!" murmured the Commandant of the Gendarmerie. "But that's all right–he has been harshly punished."

The Adjutant's wife was thinking about that punctured pocket–and the five little coins. If his pension were paid in silver, she said to herself, I'd certainly be prepared to walk behind the Wandering Jew for four or five hours.

"But what about the story?" came the complaint from every side. "The famous story!"

"The story of the Colonel and the Comtesse!"

"The Wandering Jew at Lamballe!"

"How Madame Louise de Savray got her income of 200,000 *livres*!"

"The story, Madame Lancelot, the story!"

Madame Lancelot was about to make her entrance. Although estate management is a fine career, she had not been at the dinner and was only entitled to attend the soirée. You know how many people are not let in until after the dessert.

At the moment when Madame Lancelot of the Land, duly summoned, began to speak, Sir Arthur came out of the gaming-room, with the Comtesse Louise on his arm. He had lost 1,000 *louis* to Comte Roland de Savray.

XXIV. The Death of the Wandering Jew

"I am distantly related," Madame Lancelot said, "to Monsieur Galapian, who is the Colonel's business manager. It's a queer household, where anything goes. The little one's brought up worse than a Constitutional Prince–but that doesn't concern us.

"In the Savray house, it's forbidden to mention the Wandering Jew, but everyone thinks about him. Abbé Romorantin has gone through more than 500 old books that touch upon the subject of the Wandering Jew. Monsieur Galapian comes to dine with us every Sunday. You know, of course, that there are several Wandering Jews: Isaac Laquedem, also called Ahasuerus, an old shoemaker by trade; Cartaphilus, Pontius Pilate's doorkeeper; Ozer, Herod's soldier; and others..."

"No," was the general reply. "We didn't know that."

And the Adjutant said: "This is very curious. You must introduce us to this Monsieur Galapian."

"He's a sly one, who'll make his pile up there, you'll see! So, two or three months ago, he came to dinner and said to us: 'I have the key to the puzzle.' 'What puzzle?' asked Monsieur Lancelot, who's no use away from his office–although in his office, to be sure, he's a powerful man!

"As for me, I'd already guessed that it concerned the business at Lamballe..."

At this point, Monsieur Lancelot interrupted, saying: "Incessantly occupied with administrative problems as I am, Madame Lancelot, I confess that I pay scant attention to frivolous matters. Nevertheless, it is incorrect to claim..."

Everyone told Monsieur Lancelot to shut up.

Madame Lancelot continued: "Monsieur Galapian likes little pies. We were having some. 'See here,' he says to me, 'that pedant Abbé Romorantin has found the pot of roses in Matthew Paris. It appears that the Wandering Jew dies every 100 years...' "

"Nonsense!" said the military Adjutant.

The others gave voice to their astonishment by means of various exclamations.

"I asked him," Madame Lancelot continued, "what that had to do with the Lamballe story. 'What it has to do with it,' he said, 'is that the Wandering Jew died in their house, that they looked after him while he was dying, and that he gave them a magical charm by way of payment, like Martainville's sheep's-foot.' "[17]

"Perhaps," the Adjutant observed, "he picked a hole in his pocket for them."

"What happened," Madame Lancelot continued, "is every bit as important as the matter of little Ruthael."

At which everyone cried: "What on Earth is the matter of little Ruthael?"

XXV. The Matter of Little Ruthael

"Ladies and gentlemen," Madame Lancelot of the Land went on, "there is a little girl in the Colonel's household named Lotte..."

"We know that!" The interruption came from every direction.

"A little girl named Lotte," Madame Lancelot continued, "who has been eight years old for 11 years..."

At this point, Sir Arthur burst out laughing. This Englishman was a cold fish; when he laughed, little children wept. The charms on his watch-chain represented all the Instruments of the Passion in Russian platinum.

No historian of the Restoration can explain how Médor, the Prefect's wife's poodle, had got into the salon—but Médor was there. Nothing is as brutal as a fact. Médor, on seeing Sir Arthur laugh, began howling in a lamentable fashion.

Sir Arthur stared at the dog, and Médor crouched down, moving his paw from side to side like the military Adjutant's wife playing with her fan.

We should note here that the best poet in Tours—despite working in caramel—wrote not-very-benevolent articles in the Indre's *Nain Jaune* [18] in which he accused Sir Arthur of spiritism and other funereal habits. This poet also copied personal documents for a fee. He was an all-rounder.

"Explain it as you will," Madame Lancelot continued. "Personally, I can't begin to. Little Lotte has been eight years old for the past 11 years, and that's a fact. Now, cousin Galapian had acquainted us with a rather rare item of information, which he got from Abbé Romorantin. At the time of the accident, the Wandering Jew had a daughter..."

Everyone demanded: "What accident? What accident?"

"I'm expressing myself badly. I ought to have said the catastrophe. Back there in Jerusalem, when he was condemned to wander eternally, his daughter, who was eight years old, was playing in the back of his shop. He was a widower then–it was subsequently that he espoused, in a second marriage, Queen Herodias, the widow of Herod Antipas..."

"Excuse me," objected the Commandant of the Gendarmerie. "If he is always on the move, I cannot quite imagine the internal arrangements of his household."

"I'm telling you what my cousin Galapian said," Madame Lancelot replied. "Besides, this Herodias, for her own part, is also forever on the move. She's the Wandering Jewess. Where was I?"

"The Wandering Jew's young daughter."

"Ruthael Laquedem... or, rather, Lotte..."

"What! They're the same?"

"Yes, ladies and gentlemen, and it isn't 11 years that Lotte has been eight years old but 18 centuries."

Sir Arthur burst out laughing again; on seeing that, Médor, the Prefect's wife's poodle, took refuge in copious weeping.

XXVI. The Story of Lamballe

Madame Lancelot, having firmly established these two facts–that the Wandering Jew died every 100 years, and that he had a daughter by the name of Ruthael–coughed to indicate that the dramatic part of her discourse was about to commence, and proceeded thus:

"Lamballe is an ancient city. Monsieur Lancelot claims that it was the capital of the *Ambiliati* [19] in Roman times. Everyone looks kindly upon it and the cost of living is low; I've seen a dozen eggs at three *sous*. Monsieur Lancelot, who was the famous Captain who met his death in those parts?"

"Captain La Noue,[20] Madame Lancelot."

"That's it! Well, this Captain La Noue had a Lieutenant, who had already been accused of being the Wandering Jew. Very near to the old church, perched on a rock, there was a house even older than the church. It was more than 1,000 years old. It was called the House of the Wandering Jew. It was there that Petty Lieutenant de Savray took up residence when he broke his neck by marrying Mademoiselle Louise de Louvigné, who hadn't got two pennies to rub together.

"They lived in that old house with Fanchon Honoré, who served them for the love of God, while the soldier Joli-Coeur did the heavy work. Believe it or not, they hadn't got a carriage in those days. In the town it was said that they'd eat a lot of dry bread before dying of hunger."

Here, Madame Lancelot paused to draw breath.

The Adjutant whispered: "She's common, but she's a good storyteller."

This appreciation was generally approved. Nevertheless, the President murmured: "We don't need to know the price of a dozen eggs in Lamballe! Let's stick to the point."

Madame Lancelot continued. "One evening–it was in September, like today, and it had been warm all day– the rumor went round that something funny had been seen on the hill outside the town of Andel. A traveler had appeared at the moment when the Sun was setting in the distance in the bay of Saint-Brieuc. It was a man with a long beard, on foot, who seemed three times as tall as a natural man. He was leaning on a long staff and leading by the hand a little girl so puny that the rays of the setting Sun passed clean through her body."

"That's been absoliolutely imipossible!" said Sir Arthur, shrugging his shoulders with conviction. (This was how the gentleman spoke French.)

"Look after Comtesse Louise, goddam you," muttered Madame Lancelot, "and leave us in peace." She was common, even by common standards, but she had *natural spirit*.

Sir Arthur had no need to look after Comtesse Louise, who was dancing for a second time. He gave every appearance of thinking that she was dancing well.

"And what did they do?" demanded the Commandant of the Gendarmerie, "this traveler three times as tall as nature intended and the little one the Sun's rays passed through?"

XXVII. The Dry-Bread-Savrays

"The people gathered on the old ramparts to see it," the lady of property continued, her voice involuntarily taking on mysterious inflections. "The closer the traveler came, the more obvious his weariness and the effort of his walking became. When he went into the shadow of the dale beneath the town, the little girl seemed to be a mere cloud of vapor.

"When he arrived at the town gates, he was alone.

"He stopped outside the first house and asked for hospitality. The people of Lamballe are not ungenerous, and in former times, the houses of the good Duchy of Penthevière had the reputation of always keeping their doors open and their tables laden, but a rumor ran ahead of the traveler and followed in his train: he was a traitor to God!

"Why did people say so? There was an ancient tale that claimed that the Wandering Jew sometimes died in Lamballe, in Brittany, and sometimes in the town of Ofen, in Hungary—and the house inhabited by the Dry-Bread-Savrays, as they were known, was called the House of the Wandering Jew.

"The people who had been on the old rampart to see the traveler arrive were asking one another what had become of the little girl.

"The first door remained closed. The traveler was very pale. At the second door, they said to him: 'Be on your way.' The third opened to let out a big snarling dog, which snapped at his legs.

"The traveler bowed his head in response to each refusal. From moment to moment, he was becoming paler; his knees were trembling beneath the weight of his body–but he went on his way nevertheless, knocking on doors and asking for shelter for the night.

" 'Traitor to God! Traitor to God!' Everywhere the same response.

"Soon, his tall frame was bent double; the lines of his face became hollower; the breath rattled in his chest. He took on the appearance of a man who was about to die.

"At the next-to-last house, next to the church, he knocked again. A servant opened the window and emptied a chamber-pot over his head.

"He staggered off and fell down on the threshold of the last house–which was that of the Dry-Bread-Savrays. His staff fell from his hands and thudded against the door.

"Louise, pregnant with her son, came to open it herself, because her husband was on duty at the garrison, Fanchon Honoré was at confession and Joli-Coeur at the barracks.

"Louise helped the traveler to his feet and took him by the hand, despite all those who were crying: 'Traitor to God! Traitor to God!' She helped him over the step at the threshold, and laid him down in her own bed..."

"But you know," said the Commandant of the Gendarmerie, at this point, "I don't disapprove of that!"

"Clever! Clever!" said the Adjutant. "She had an idea!"

Everyone wanted to know the opinion of Sir Arthur, who replied frankly: "That's been ray-markabarbly stewpid!"

"It is nevertheless the case," the Public Prosecutor put in, "that the Traitor to God is in the home of the Dry-

Breads. This is interesting. Let's see what happens next."

XXVIII. One Night's Secret

Louise was dancing for the third time, this time with her husband—and if you knew how happy she seemed...!

While dancing, she murmured: "Our Paul will scold us when we go back."

They made a charming couple. The guests of the Prefecture smiled at the sight of them. Sir Arthur never stopped staring at Comtesse Louise's eyes.

Madame Lancelot went on:

"The lights burned all night in the house of the Dry-Bread-Savrays. The husband came home; Joli-Coeur and Fanchon Honoré too. Each of them suspected that a death was about to take place; even so, the door remained bolted. No one was sent to look for a doctor or a priest.

"Monsieur Lancelot and I were living next door..."

"Ah!" the Commandant of the Gendarmerie put in. "Then, the servant who emptied the chamber-pot was yours!"

The lady of property reddened slightly, and replied: "Don't talk to me about servants! All night, there were comings and goings in the Savray house. We heard moaning and groaning, and muttered prayers. Then, around dawn, there was a masculine cry of joy, mingled with the crying of a child.

"When the Sun came up, the traveler came out, upright and steady on his strong legs.

"He was alone. He went down the mountain and steered eastwards. He was lost to our view in the valley. When we caught sight of him again, climbing the far slope, he was holding the hand of a little girl whose graceful and diaphanous body was pierced by the rays of the rising Sun.

"That very day, a letter arrived at the house of Lamballe's Notary. One of Comtesse Louise's aunts had died at Landerneau. There was a large inheritance.

"At the military headquarters, another letter arrived, which announced Lieutenant Roland de Savray's promotion to Captain.

"A third letter came to the Prefecture at Saint-Brieuc. King Louis XVIII had remembered his god-daughter Louise and conferred the title of Comte on her husband.

"Monsieur Lancelot and I discharged our servant, because the stroke of luck could have fallen our way. Now, it'll be necessary to wait for 100 years..."

"And then," said Monsieur Lancelot, "it will be the turn of Ofen, in Hungary.

"The best way," concluded Commandant Lamadou, "is to have a good heart every day."

XXIX. To the Fire!

It was midnight. Tours in Touraine is two hours ahead of Paris.[21] Midnight is the perfect moment at Prefecture balls. The punch was fuming. The Public Prosecutor was hobnobbing with Monsieur Lamadou. The Adjutant had turned out to be a waltzer.

Sir Arthur was staring at Comtesse Louise. On reflection, Vicomte Paul probably had good reason to detest the English; Sir Arthur's gaze was cold, scornful and fearsome.

In truth, the world had good reason to snipe at the Savrays. Their good fortune was excessive; they had found paradise on Earth.

Comtesse Louise, in the arms of her beloved Roland, had left the ballroom to take the air on the terrace. There, among the perfumes ascending from the flowerbeds, they talked about the future–which is to say, of Paul, the child so dear to their hearts. They had a profound affection for one another, but Paul was like the hearth of that beautiful tenderness.

They were interrupted in the middle of their intimate conversation by the cawing of a crow. This was Sir Arthur, who said in French:

"Lewk! Lewk! I begged yew! Lewk at that beeyewtiful spectacle! I believed that it's been a boreal aurora! Indeed!"

Indeed, the sky was ardently tinted in the most extraordinary fashion, but the purple fire was not glowing in the north.

The terrace filled up with curiosity-seekers within an eye-blink.

"It's a fire!" cried the Commandant of the Gendarmerie, at first glance.

"And a terrible fire!" added the Prefect.

"In which direction?"

Comtesse Louise already felt her heart squeezed. She felt her husband's arm quiver beneath her own.

"In the west," said the President.

"Towards Luynes..."

"One might be mistaken," added the Adjutant, "but one would swear that it's Colonel de Savray's house."

Louise stifled a cry of terror. "Paul!" she gasped. "My son!"

As Roland, already mad with anxiety, ran forward, a soldier covered in dust and running with sweat came out of the Prefecture. It was the hussar Joli-Coeur.

"My Colonel," he said, "the barracks have been roused. What can be done has been done. Come."

At the same time, the tocsin was sounded by the churches, and the awakened town let out a long cry of alarm:

"To the fire! To the fire! The Luynes road! The home of Colonel Comte de Savray."

XXX. The Conflagration

The calèche was drawn along at a furious gallop by its two horses. Comte Roland supported the swooning Comtesse in his arms. On the road, they met hussars who were making all possible haste, breathless firemen, and crowds of curiosity seekers trotting and strolling along.

"Paul!" murmured the Comtesse. "No one told me about Paul!"

Behind the calèche, in the place normally occupied by the footman, there was a man warmly wrapped up in an ample cloak. This man leaned down sometimes, lifting his hood in order to gaze at Comtesse Louise. At such moment, one would have been able to recognize the blond hair of Sir Arthur, gleaming in the moonlight.

Chivalrous self-sacrificial gestures are sometimes encountered among the English. Perhaps Sir Arthur had chosen this means of arriving more rapidly to do battle with the conflagration. He was quite a character.

On clearing the poplars, an awesome and horrible tableau was revealed. The villa was nothing but an immense sheaf of flame, illuminating the peaceful countryside, where there had formerly been nothing but good fortune.

The hussars were attacking the fire, and how valiantly! Everyone who has ever seen our French soldiers at grips with fiery tempests has admired the sublime rapture of human bravery! They could be seen throwing themselves forward, as if the charge had sounded, as if the enemy were flesh and blood; they could be seen attacking, with heads lowered, the fulgurant colossus. The majority were thrust back at the first impact, but some few got through: active demons and salamanders, black within the red furnace.

"Paul!" cried Comtesse Louise. "Is Paul safe?"

Colonel Roland threw himself out of the calèche and ran up the hill. Sir Arthur leapt down and followed him, leaving Louise no more than semi-conscious in the carriage.

As the injured passed by, carried on stretchers, Louise dared not make inquiries, but she heard someone say: "There's only the child upstairs, at the very top of the house!"

The child! Her Paul! Her heart!

Louise clasped her hands together, pronounced the name of God, and sank into unconsciousness.

XXXI. The Colonel's Father

At the very top of the house, there was a solitary room, from which the view was splendid. From there, a veritable panorama unrolled before the eye. The Colonel Comte de Savray had made that room into his study. He often slept there.

After the grand dinner in the pavilion, given in imitation of the gala at the Prefecture, Vicomte Paul–who "was Papa"–had wanted to do exactly as his father did, and sleep in the study.

All Vicomte Paul's guests were a trifle *animated*. If Wellington had shown up, there would have been ructions. Wellington, faithful to his legendary prudence, had failed to show up. Vicomte Paul was allowed to do as he wished. Fanchon and Joli-Coeur, after having put him into the paternal bed, gloriously happy, had retired themselves.

Now, Vicomte Paul had heard it said that his father "locked himself away in his study." As soon as he was sure that he was alone, he got up and went, barefoot, to bolt the door. After that, tranquil and sure of having conscientiously imitated his father, he lay down again to snore like a Vicomte who has given himself and others an exceedingly good dinner.

Joli-Coeur and Fanchon the nurse chatted for a while. They talked about the strange story, recounted at the Prefecture by Madame Lancelot. It seems that this story was true, since Joli-Coeur and Fanchon, eye-witnesses to the events, gave no lie to the bizarre tale that we have heard. But it seems, too, that Madame Lancelot did not know everything, because Fanchon and Joli-Coeur were talking about a misfortune...

They were saying: "What a pity! A man who has been, for 60 years, the most worthy lord in the land!"

As we have no reason to keep the secret, we shall briefly explain the misfortune in question. They were talking about old Monsieur de Savray, the Colonel's father.

This honest gentleman had come to live in Lamballe with the young household. After that mysterious night, which was followed by so much prosperity–the night when the traveler had arrived dying, only to go away again full of strength and life–the gentleman had become unrecognizable. One could not say that he had lost his head, because he reasoned perfectly well, but–in Fanchon's expression–"a devil had got into his body." He scandalized the town with his excesses; he blasphemed like a damned soul; he drank like a sponge; he stole... yes, you read it correctly, he stole like a brigand.

He stole! An old gentleman! He did even worse. I do not know, in truth, how Madame Lancelot remained ignorant of it. If she had known, what a success she would have had at the Prefecture! The fact is that the Savrays had left Lamballe a few days after the passage of the fantastic traveler.

One night, the Colonel's father had disappeared. The gendarmes...

My God, yes! Joli-Coeur and Fanchon thought that the gentleman had ended his days in prison. And Fanchon said, while shaking her head: "When *one* shows himself, *the other* isn't far away."

One was Isaac Laquedem; *the other* was Ozer, the soldier who extended to the Savior of the World, dying on the cross, the lance at whose tip was the sponge soaked in vinegar. Both Jews, both Wanderers–and Immortals, due to the curse of the Lord Jesus.

Did Fanchon Honoré think, then, that the elder Monsieur de Savray, who turned to evil in his old age, was the victim of some curse, put upon him by *one* or *the other*...?

XXXII. During the Fire

There is a peculiar little animal that lives on our shores called a hermit crab. It is a crustacean that is intermediate in form between a crab and a lobster; in size, it is much smaller than a shrimp, and it is good for absolutely nothing. Its way of life involves killing mollusks in order to eat them and then to take possession of their homes.

The wretched Ozer, the third sort of Wandering Jew, is similar in kind. He has the terrible power of introducing his unworthy soul into the bodies of honest men, as if hitching a lift. A lamb, white as snow until 59 years of age, can end up in the Court of Assizes before turning 60 when he has the soldier Ozer in his body.

How many catastrophes human life is exposed to!

"When *one* shows himself, *the other* isn't far away!" Fanchon Honoré had pronounced these words, sure of her facts.

This merits explanation.

According to some worthy authorities, the legend of the Wandering Jew is nothing but a figment of the popular imagination, recalling the Savior's merciful promise of the eventual repentance of the Jewish people. According to other authors, equally reliable, the Jew–or rather the three Jews–expiating by eternal weariness the outrageous crime of having insulted the Son of God, really exist.

It seems certain, according to them, that this diabolical soldier Ozer, Wandering Jew Number Three, travels through the same regions as Ahasuerus, called Laquedem, Wandering Jew Number One. As for Cartaphilus, Pontius Pilate's porter and Wandering Jew Number Two, he does not disturb the world very much.

Let us return to Vicomte Paul's guests.

While Fanchon and Joli-Coeur were discussing the Lamballe adventure, already long past, wondering what the traveler whose shadow had been cast by the setting Sun might have been doing in the meantime, Good Abbé Romorantin was saying his prayers before going to bed. Monsieur Galapian, nicknamed Addition, was occupied with another arithmetical process of which men of business are said to be particularly fond, which goes by the name of subtraction. Unlike theft, which is also an arithmetical operation, but has a bad reputation, decent and proper subtraction discreetly places its moral consequences in a savings-bank. Monsieur Galapian was a thrifty man.

Abbé Romorantin and Monsieur Galapian both had rooms on the second floor of the villa. In the absence of the owners, there was no one on the first floor. On the ground floor, all the household servants, put into a good mood by the dinner in the pavilion, continued making merry. By the grace of God, there was merrymaking everywhere: in the kitchen, the pantry and the stables. Sapajou tried to walk on the ceiling like a fly, but could not do it.

At about 10 p.m., everyone lay down to sleep, some in their beds and some under the table. No one can be responsible for a house in this state, and those who go to balls at the Prefecture do not know what risks they are running.

Given the mysterious milieu in which our story takes place, one might suspect that some sorcery was involved, but there was actually no need. The least little thing was sufficient: a candle fallen over; a lantern broken; a lamp overturned. The Colonel's charming villa was a wooden-framed building.

At about 10:30 p.m., the sleepers awoke with a start, choked by thick smoke. They lost time rubbing their eyes. They were still hung over; they began accusing one another, arguing, losing their tempers. The fire took firmer hold.

In the end, they got out. The flames were already shooting from the first floor windows.

Fortunately, the right wing, where Vicomte Paul normally slept, was the furthest from the fire. Fanchon and Joli-Coeur, the child's two bodyguards, were still asleep. Several people thought of waking them up, but as they did so, cries of alarm sounded from the second floor. It was Monsieur Galapian, imploring help for himself and his savings. He was at his bedroom window in his nightshirt. He called to each one by name, taking God as his witness, although he only believed in the Devil. He promised heaps of gold.

Ladders were set up. Vicomte Paul's quarters were still not under threat. They took the time to save Galapian—and, while they were at it, the good Abbé Romorantin, who immediately ran towards his pupil's room. It was he who woke Joli-Coeur and Fanchon.

"Vicomte Paul's bed is empty!" he cried, in anguish.

Everyone had forgotten the poor child's final whim.

No one remembered that Vicomte Paul had wanted to sleep in the Colonel's room—at the very top of the house that now resembled an immense funeral-pyre.

At first there was a stupefied silence, then a general cry of distress.

"Paul! Paul! Madame la Comtesse's treasure! The Colonel's only son!"

XXXIII. The Assaults

Monsieur Galapian could hardly maintain his composure. He was still shouting more loudly than anyone else, because he had lost one of his slippers.

Like a madman, the brave Abbé Romorantin threw himself towards the fiery staircase that was almost burned through.

Joli-Coeur had already set up the slaters' ladder and was clambering up. A window-frame fell upon on him and cast him back down to the courtyard, badly bruised. Fanchon was on her knees, praying and beating her breast. Everyone was in sore distress, but that was no help at all to Vicomte Paul.

At every instant, they expected to see the poor child's handsome face appear at the window of the attic, white with terror amid the vivid red of the flames. But the window remained shut, and there was not the least sign of Vicomte Paul.

Was he asleep in the midst of all this clamor, above that flaming furnace?

Joli-Coeur leapt on to a horse, with neither saddle not bridle, and raced towards the town. He was an old soldier. He woke the barracks before going on to warn the Colonel.

The hussars began to arrive first, mostly out of uniform. Four hundred semi-clad men mounted the first assault on the conflagration. It might as well have been a fort defended by Cossacks!

The fire was victorious. Thirty injured men were sprawled on the paving-stones of the courtyard.

The firemen arrived next. These heroes are long accustomed to telling eager listeners the tales of their modest prowess. For them, such exploits as this are everyday affairs; they are the best man for the job and are men of iron or stone. Firemen! I have seen men laugh as they pronounce the names of these sublimely dutiful soldiers.

Water shot forth in sparkling jets and fell upon the stoked-up brazier. It was like a colossal fuse covering the hill with its fire-powder. Then, the initial moment having passed, the fire paled and the smoke became thicker.

The firemen attempted the scaling-ladder in their turn, for everyone around them was saying: "In the attic room, at the very top, the son of the house is in bed asleep."

The firemen climbed up, cooler, more careful and more ingenious than the hussars. They got up higher, but they came to a dead end.

There were more injured men on the pavement of the courtyard, and the brave men who had directed the rescue-party said in low voices:

"The Colonel's child is lost!"

XXXIV. The Staircase

Where, then, was Colonel Comte Roland de Savray? He had been seen to leave the calèche and run up the hill. No one had noticed the blond-bearded Sir Arthur climbing up behind him.

Comte Roland was nowhere to be seen. They searched for him in vain. The absence of the master in such desperate circumstances was a strange thing.

Comtesse Louise was still in a faint in her calèche. No one was watching over her; the coachman and the valets were at the fire.

The hussars and foremen were preparing for one last attempt, this time working together. The central staircase had been exposed following successive collapses; they hoped to make use of it. For the benefit of anyone who has never seen the outcome of the splendid follies of courage, this was an extravagant enterprise.

The regimental trumpets sounded as if for the charge, and two intrepid battalions–the hussars and the foremen–flung themselves upon the blazing building.

At that moment, Comtesse Louise recovered consciousness.

She could see the black angels walking into the fire... vanquishing the fire, we might say, for the two rescue-parties penetrated as far as the staircase.

But the staircase collapsed, hurling a column of turbulent sparks into the sky.

There was a general exclamation as profound as a death-rattle–then a cry of joyful astonishment.

Everyone, including the mother, saw a man–was it a man?–appear at the window of the attic.

The man was exceptionally tall. He wore a long beard sprinkled with particles of ash; he had a long staff in his hand. In his arms, he was carrying a child clad only in a white nightshirt.

And the child seemed to be asleep.

Comtesse Louise extended her trembling arms. She could not speak, but it was as if her entire heart went out to God.

The man put his leg over the balcony. The blaze lit the scene better than the summer Sun in brought daylight. He was calm and collected. Was that a cloud of smoke or a human form behind him?

Many of the people who were there, quivering and hopeful, pronounced the name of Lotte. And some among them, who knew the story of Lamballe, added:

"*The Wandering Jew's daughter!*"

XXXV. Sir Arthur's Disappearance

Once more, where was Comte Roland de Savray: the master of the house; the Colonel; the father?

The staircase was no more, and the flames were licking the surfaces of the blackened walls. The man on the balcony with the spark-sprinkled beard began to move, to come down. He used the debris of the walls like stepping-stones; his pace was slow but sure. The child still seemed to be asleep in his arms.

He reached the earth of the courtyard. A great circle formed around him, composed of people full of admiration–and of fear.

Joli-Coeur and Fanchon kissed the hem of his smoldering overcoat. Abbé Romorantin stammered a prayer of thanks. Monsieur Galapian dared not ask the man to go back to look for his slipper, although he wanted to.

The man crossed the courtyard and went down the hill. It was obvious where he was going, and everyone said: "The mother! The poor mother! How happy she will be!"

While the man was seen at close range, nothing could be seen of that indecisive form that resembled little Lotte. But when he drew further away, as he descended the slope, the light of the conflagration illuminated a vague vision that seemed to sway in the night-breeze. The vision was following the man.

The man gave the child back to his mother but did not pause to take heed of her thankful gestures. He continued on his way. Eventually, he disappeared behind the poplars.

At that moment, Colonel Roland de Savray suddenly appeared beside the calèche. There was something strange and unusual about him, but what? No one was able to determine precisely what it was.

"The lad's saved–so much the better!" he said, in a voice that was certainly the Colonel's, although there was something in it like an echo of Sir Arthur's guttural accent. All this had put him to a great deal of trouble!

The Comtesse paused in her fervent hugging of Vicomte Paul, who had woken up smiling. That voice wounded her as deeply as the words it spoke.

Was it really Comte Roland who spoke in this manner? The same Comte Roland that had such a passionate affection for his only son?

Joli-Coeur and Fanchon exchanged glances.

"The old gentleman–the Colonel's father–had that voice in Lamballe..." the hussar began.

"When all that was honest in him turned to mischief!" the nurse finished.

The Colonel, meanwhile, yawned, clicking his jaw in the process.

"Well," he said, "let's go get a room at the inn. I don't care about the house–it's insured!"

The Comtesse drew away, in order not to have the slightest contact with him. She was astonished to feel nothing now but cold repugnance for the man she had loved so much. She clasped Vicomte Paul tightly to her bosom; as he said in a low voice:

"What's become of Papa? It's certainly Papa, but I don't want to hug him."

By the following day, the Colonel had entirely lost that English accent–but Comtesse Louise and her son were very sad, without knowing why.

Sir Arthur had disappeared, and was never seen again in Tours in Touraine.

XXXVI. A German

The snow was a scourge, driven by the northwest wind. The enormous trees, extending their long naked branches, were bright on one side, whitened by snow, while their trunks became blacker by contrast on the other.

It was the morning of a January day. The woodcutters were already abroad, on footpaths innocent of any track, covered with a dazzling tablecloth of snow. They clapped their numbed hands behind their backs, and hid their reddened noses in their bosoms. In the woods, they could hear the sounds made by the Baron von Pfifferlackentrontonstein, former privy councilor to the former sovereign prince of Rudelsigmarienthal-Tartempoeffen-Topinambourg-Lapinstadt–who had recently sold his vast estates to the King of Prussia for a tobacconist's shop. (Such is fate!)

It was bitterly cold. The Baron was in a very bad mood, as much because he had lost his position as because he had lost the track of an old stag, which was even shrewder than he was. He whipped his horse, who could do no more, and cursed his dogs, who had been blinded by the snow and had lost the scent, having contracted a cold in the head. He said hurtful things to his huntsman, Fritz, and looked forward to the quarrel he would have on his return with his beloved wife, Baroness Wilhelmina-Concordia-Charlotte-Françoise-Petronilla-Angelica-Urania von Pfifferlackentrontonstein, born in the palace of Choumakre, with a 14th share of the minor Diet of Srzghw.

So we are no longer in Tours in Touraine, then? No. We have crossed the whole of France and passed over the Rhine. We are traveling in Germany. We are passing through the famous Hercynian forest–the Hartz, if you prefer the name given to it by geographers and charcoal-burners.

On this pale morning, we are passing beneath the giant fir-trees where so many phantoms have been seen. The people here know that the dead go swiftly. This snow is the winding-sheet of the eternal ballad. This wind carries the sighs of specters. This is German gaiety–hurrah!

This has the feel of a cemetery–hurrah! That's true poetry for you. These Huns are merry companions. Hurrah for shrouds, coffins, bones, fleshless skulls, tombs that open wide! The Germans are enjoying themselves: hurrah! hurrah! The Prussian Fatherland forever! [22]

XXXVII. The Sunken Path

The path led downwards, winding around the steep slopes of Mount Andreasberg, famous for the restlessness of its dead woodcutters (hurrah!) and also for its silver mines, a kilometer deep. In the background, there were bare and jagged mountain peaks, their crags jumbled chaotically. In the foreground, the immense forest extended, the trees on its horizon taking on the appearance of old men's powdered wigs.

A man went along the footpath silently, dejected and wearied by the sort of chronic fatigue that no longer has the strength to complain.

On our French roads, you will sometimes find a poor wounded soldier limping along in the same fashion, his bag on his shoulder, looking enviously at every carriage that passes by. But our man was not limping. He stood up straight and his pace was strong and steady. All his lassitude was in the sad resignation of his facial expression.

He supported himself with a long staff and held a little girl by the hand. Both of them seemed insensible to the harsh chill of the weather. They were not talking to one another. The man gravely doffed his hat before the crosses situated at the crossroads, and the little girl made the sign of the cross.

When an abrupt mountain ridge silhouetted the travelers against the horizon of the Hartz, there was a strange illusion. Seen from below, the man was sharply outlined in black, against the snowy summits, while the child seemed as diaphanous as vapor. Through her frail and charming body, the azure peaks of the Andreasberg could be seen.

At the bottom of the slope, the path, narrowed and framed by two steep banks, led into the forest. A stone column bore the following inscription: *Andreasberg Mine: Three Wells Road.*

"I recall," the man said, "that I have been in these parts before."

"And what were you looking for, so far away from him and her, Father?" said the young woman–we do not know quite how to describe her: she was a child, but she was also a young woman.

The traveler had no time to reply. The wind carried the fanfare of a hunt, blotting out the loud baying of a pack of stag hounds in the woods. Galloping horses were soon heard, reverberating all the more sonorously in the frozen ground–then the Baron's voice crying in German, with Stentorian [23] force:

"Tally ho! Tally ho! Tally ho!"

The Baron's voice was hoarse, and gave abundant evidence of his bad mood.

Suddenly, at the end of the sunken path, a slender and graceful hind appeared, running flat out and turning her pretty head to the rear. It was she who had given the slip to the stag hounds, and the Baron had sworn that she would pay with the forfeit of her life.

The hind bore down upon our travelers; they moved aside to let her pass, the man to the right and the child to the left, and each of them saw that there were tears in the other's eyes.

"Tally ho! Tally ho! Tally ho!"

The trumpets signaled a sighting. The dogs bayed.

The traveler and the little girl had, however, retaken their place in the middle of the road, which they blocked in its entirety. The dogs arrived in their turn at full speed, and behind the dogs, the Baron and his hunters.

"Get back!" he cried from a distance, the moment he saw the man with the staff. "The road's mine!"

The man continued placidly on his way.

"Get back, beggar! I'm Baron von Pfifferlacken-trontonstein, former Privy Councilor to the former Sovereign Prince of Rudelsigmarienthal-Tartemp..."

He had not time enough to pronounce such noble names; the Baron was still at Tartemp... when the dogs, less prolix, were already throwing themselves upon our traveler. They were strong dogs, known for ten leagues around to be as vicious as mad wolves.

"Bite him!" said the huntsman in a low voice. "Kiss! Kiss! Kiss!" [24]

A fine tumble he was hoping for, this huntsman.

There was indeed a tumble, but it was the dogs who took it, rolling as they fell over one another, as far as the hooves of the horses, as if 30 robust hands–there were 30 of them–had taken each of them by the scruff of the neck and thrown them into the air.

"What the Devil...!"

The traveler had merely lifted his long staff. He continued on his way as if nothing had happened, with his little girl at his side.

"What the blasted Devil...!"[25]

The dogs, in being thrust back, bumped into the horses, which reared back. kicked out and turned tail, hurtling down the sunken path as if the Devil were indeed at their heels.

The Baron threatened the dogs, the horses, the travelers and even the hind–who had gone to meet up with her stag–as best he could. Nothing came of it.

The records of the era report that the Baron, eventually giving way to a fit of impatience, discharged both barrels of his rifle and a brace of pistols at the ill-met traveler–who merely shrugged his shoulders. The bullets fell into the snow.

Seeing this, the Baron went on his way, and did not stop until he was at the steps of his schloss. He beat the Baroness for the first time in his life, even though she had been born in the palace of Choumakre. Afterwards, he got the habit, which became second nature to him.

XXXVIII. The Three Wells

The Baron was wrong to beat his wife; that is not the way to behave. But if the Sovereign Prince of (the name is above) had not sold his estates to the King of Prussia for a tobacconist's shop, no traveler would ever have dared to show the Baron such scant respect, in which case the Baron would never have battered his wife. It is necessary to concede the case of *force majeure*–as it often is in Prussia.[26]

The man and the little girl arrived at the place called Three Wells, which formed one of the entrances to the great gallery of the mines of Andreasberg.

"Go down, Ruthael," the man said to the child, "and come back to tell me what you have seen."

The little girl got into the basket and sounded the bell. The basket descended into the night.

While the basket made its descent, a soft voice emerged from the well, saying:

"In the name of the Father, the Son and the Holy Spirit, Good Lord, pardon my father..."

The man continued his march, eating a piece of stale bread and drinking from his water-bottle.

XXXIX. The Andreasberg Mine

There is an immense subterranean city that has thousands of streets, public squares, churches, palaces, canals, lakes, boutiques, theatres, hospitals and ballrooms. Berlin could be rebuilt in silver with all the wealth that has come out of this inexhaustible mine.

In the suburbs of this enchanted city, 900 meters beneath the ground, two men were working the ore with pickaxes, beside a pool of water as dark as the Acheron. Their lanterns were burning sadly at their feet. Both paused to wipe the sweat from their brows.

"Friend," said one to the other, "let's talk some more about that dream we both had."

"All right," replied the other. "It's an antidote to fatigue. It seems to me that the dream is a measure of fresh air, the perfume of flowers and the gentle rays of the Sun."

They sat down side by side and the first went on:

"My name is Sir Arthur..."

"But I won a great many *louis* from a gentleman of that name," the other put in, "who certainly wasn't you."

"You're probably right, friend; that wasn't me. At least... there are times when I'm not sure of my own identity. You see, it's my belief that someone has taken my body–and it's madness to believe the impossible, isn't it?"

His companion shook his head slowly. "Myself, I was a Comte... and a Colonel. I had a wife that I loved, a child I adored. That must be true, since the memory fills my eyes with tears."

"And someone has taken your body, too–isn't that so?" Sir Arthur queried.

"Yes. One night, my château caught fire. This man... but it was he who called himself Sir Arthur!"

The other miner was deep in thought, his head slumped over his breast. "Then it's the same person," he said, "that has taken both our bodies!"

They looked at one another hopelessly. Something was weighing on their numbed minds.

"Let's go," said the thick voice of an overseer. "Look–these two madmen are slacking again! To work, rogues! You don't earn the bread that you eat!"

The two poor miners obediently took up their picks and set to work again.

A beautiful young girl, dressed like the daughter of a wealthy house, appeared behind the overseer. The overseer turned to her and said:

"You see, Mademoiselle, it's necessary to watch these two ceaselessly. They'd get a rap of my hammer if you weren't here. Here's the one who thinks he's an English baronet–that's Sir Arthur. Does he look like one, eh?"

The young girl came closer. The gaze of her lovely eyes fell upon the second miner, who shivered.

"This one," the overseer went on, shrugging his shoulders, "is a Colonel, French–a Colonel of hussars..."

"Colonel Comte Roland de Savray," murmured the beautiful young girl.

The overseer burst out laughing and gave the poor man a rude shove as his pick attacked a block of ore.

But as he worked, the poor man said to himself:

"Lotte! I've seen Lotte! Is there truth, then, beneath the cloud that dulls my mind?"

XL. To Paris

At the moment when our traveler, after having dined on the move on dry bread and water, returned to Three Wells, the basket brought the little girl back up to the surface. She had resumed the form and frail appearance of a child.

"Father," she said, "they're both down there. I would not have recognized them, for what remains of their souls is confined in the bodies of rejects–but they still have soul enough to remember vaguely, and are suffering cruelly."

The traveler did not stop to listen.

"We're going to Paris," he said.

"To Paris!" she exclaimed, as a joyful smile lit up the pallor of her face. "So I'll see them again–her and him!"

"Ruthael," said the traveler in a whisper, "I have questioned the Angel. God will allow you to choose between your father and your spouse..."

"Me! Leave you!" cried the child, dissolving into tears.

Without pausing, the traveler lifted her up in his arms and pressed her to his heart.

"Ozer is there," he said. "The infamous Ozer! I've learned here what I wanted to know. God is merciful. Every good deed diminishes my pain. Let's go to do good and fight evil."

Ruthael, who had collected herself, murmured:

"Good Lord, pardon my father, in the name of the Father, the Son and the Holy Spirit."

XLI. Paul the Student

We are in Paris. Time is like the Wandering Jew; it moves on and on...

Time has moved on.

Comtesse Louise was still beautiful, but very sad and very pale. You would scarcely have recognized Vicomte Paul in the proud young man with the melancholy expression, who went out twice a day to the Collège Henri IV and came back twice a day, alone, distancing himself from the joyful mischief of his schoolmates. Vicomte Paul called himself plain Monsieur Paul. Only Fanchon Honoré ever made the mistake of occasionally giving him his former title.

Misfortune had put heavy thoughts into that young head. Although Paul no longer laughed as he once did, he labored with all his might. He had a goal. He labored in order to support his mother.

What! Did Comtesse Louise de Savray, that young woman who was so rich and so brilliant, and above all so fortunate, need to be supported now? And what could an adolescent, a pupil of the Collège Henri IV, do for the god-daughter of King Louis XVIII?

King Louis XVIII had been dead for years. The 200,000 *livres* income was God knows where. Comtesse Louise lived in a small third-floor apartment on the Rue de l'Ouest. She wore a widow's weeds, although Colonel Comte Roland de Savray was not dead.

Whenever our friend Paul went back into the Collège Henri IV, he embraced his mother, and both of them often wept.

XLII. The Colonel's Litanies

The other guests at the Prefecture had mostly prospered. The Prefect had become a State Councilor; the Public Prosecutor was on the bench of the Court of Appeal; Madame Lancelot of the Land and her husband, Monsieur Lancelot, had been promoted to the Ministry of Finance. Some of the male dancers had lost their hair and become serious men; some of the female dancers had put on weight, a hundred per cent or more. The Adjutant had lost nothing.

It was the month of July in the year 1830. Because General Lamadou (the former Commandant of the Gendarmerie of Tours in Touraine) was throwing a big party on the occasion of the marriage of his niece to Monsieur Galapian, all of our old Tourainean acquaintances had naturally come together again.

But let us pause to say a few words about Monsieur Galapian.

Monsieur Galapian, as we have said, was a skillful man and a good accountant. He was no longer so scornful of the Good Lord since he had rounded out his pile to the extent of a guaranteed annual income of 60,000 francs. No one, he freely admitted, had ever doubted his probity. I can well believe it! He had certainly sorted out the business of the de Savray house, and put them in good order. He did a good deal for the poor in taking care of their meager wages. Madame Lancelot cited him to her supernumeraries as an example of what could be achieved by the compatibility of mind and conduct.

"Do you know what they're saying?" she exclaimed, as she made her entrance that evening. "Your servant, ladies; compliments to your husbands. They'll make a charming couple, won't they? Do you know what they're saying?"

In Paris, as in Tours, Madame Lancelot was held in high esteem as a source of news. Since those times, the Havas Agency [27] and petty newspapers have depreciated that kind of talent. A circle formed around Madame Lancelot, who went on:

"Business isn't good, commerce is shaky, the bourgeoisie are discontented. We're dancing above a volcano!"

"Permit me, my lady and friend," General Lamadou put in. "I shall not tolerate the manifestation of opposition in my own home."

Galapian said: "I'm a man of order, but at the Bourse today, I sold and sold and sold. I'll buy it all back at half price the day after the revolution–that's the way I'm thinking."

There was an admiring murmur, and the ladies murmured in the ear of the General's niece:

"That's a fine chap, Léocadie, and you'll be very happy!"

"Do you know what's being spread around?" Madame Lancelot went on, impetuously. "It's all about politics! We don't need to worry about politics. There'll always be leaders, won't there? I want to talk to you about a boy... the poor devil! We knew him smartly turned-out. Do you remember way back, in Tours, when they cried out on the steps of the Prefecture: 'Colonel Comte de Savray's carriage!' "

"Oh, yes!" said the Adjutant's wife, pouting. "That unfortunate man..."

"Irresponsible!" said the former Tourainean Public Prosecutor.

"A cockroach!" [28] murmured Galapian. "I predicted it!"

"And you have done everything you could to save him, Stanislas!" murmured young Léocadie. Monsieur Galapian's first name was Stanislas.

There was some dry coughing, doubtless intended to express warm appreciation, then the rosary fell apart:

"A drinker!" Lancelot declared.

"A gambler!"

"A bravo!"

"A bad lot!"

"A monster!"

This litany was in honor of poor Comte Roland de Savray.

XLIII. Monsieur Galapian's Good Side

"Very well," Madame Lancelot went on. "And his Comtesse Louise also got into difficulties. There were no more dances with the general staff for her. The Colonel has left her in the lurch–that's an old story. He has eaten up an income of 200,000 a year. He has lived liked Punch.[29] You know all that. But what you don't know is that he's going to be brought before a court-martial..."

"A court-martial!" was generally echoed.

"A court-martial! To be cashiered, shot, hanged, guillotined, broken on the wheel!"

"For what crime?"

"For every crime! Theft, fraud, cheating at cards, outraging public morals, assassinations, poisonings, arsons, drownings, forgeries..."

"But you know," said young Lamadou, the General's younger brother and an Advocate in the Royal Court, "it'll be a very jolly affair!"

"And the unfortunate wife?" one of the groom's female cousins ventured, timidly.

"There's one," murmured Madame Lancelot, "who's always wool-gathering."[30]

The cousin went on:

"And the child? He must be a young man now..."

"Vicomte Paul," Monsieur Galapian put in. "I'll take him into one of my offices, if he shows enough aptitude."

"Oh, Stanislas," sighed Léocadie, rapt with admiration. "You have a good heart."

General Lamadou wiped away a tear.

A valet announced:

"Monsieur Lunat, Member of the Institute!"[31]

XLIV. Extraordinary Prophecies

Little Doctor Lunat was no longer mad–quite the contrary–and he had grown fat. This is why: having ceased to take himself for the Wandering Jew, he had given up walking entirely, in order to compensate for his 1,800-year excursion. He was as round as a bowling-ball and had taken his place directly among the benefactors of his century. The affair of the crocodile was famed throughout Europe. Magi came from London and Moscow to adore Doctor Lunat. The Academy of Sciences had added to its luster by taking him into its bosom.

Apart from the crocodile cure, Doctor Lunat had many other happy outcomes to his scientific credit. He was the inventor of the Tragic system of treatment and Alexandrine douches.

The Tragic system–of which much use has since been made–cures madmen by the patient and reasonable ingestion of a complete tragedy by Voltaire, which won a second prize at the Conservatory;[32] it is fed to the patient, by day and by night, until he dies. Alexandrine douches, although less well known, have also rendered sterling service. The patient is walled up in a cell decorated with famous couplets, placed in such a position that an acoustic conduit can pour into his ear the various verses of the *Henriade*.[33] In sum, the two treatments constitute the great exasperatory school. When nothing comes of them, people are plunged into a session of the Chamber at Versailles.[34]

Nothing could be further from our thoughts than to list the innumerable cures obtained with the aid of these ingenious methods. Doctor Lunat is no charlatan, to imitate those healers who insert the recommendations of ancient spinsters and the effusive thanks of Hospodars [35] into their newspaper advertisements.

"Ladies," he said, bowing to the circle, "I'm founding a hospital for sages, with an initial capital of a mere three million. The speculation is based on the calculation that all madmen will flock there in order to turn their lives around. My compliments to the bride and groom; Galapian belongs to the shark family; it will be a long..."

"What? What!" the groom attempted to protest.

"My Stanislas, a shark!" said Léocadie, indignantly.

"It's a serious analogy," the fat little Doctor replied. "Science can never be offensive. General Lamadou belongs to the family of oxen..."

"I'll be damned!" said Lamadou. "That's how you think of the Gendarmerie?"

"Don't get carried away! Madame Lancelot belongs to the shrike species..." [36]

"Now, then! Monsieur Lunat...!"

"I'm definitely a parrot myself," the Doctor put in, proudly. "Did you know that Abbé Romorantin has finally resolved the great problem? The Abbé Romorantin who was formerly with you in the Savray household. That one could give testimony, if anyone ever accuses you of not being a brave man; he never speaks of you without tears in his eyes."

"Good old Romorantin!" murmured Galapian.

"I pay him 200 francs a month to serve as my pen, my memory, my spectacles and my genius," the Doctor went on. "It's expensive. Do you know that he uses his money to pay for the food and lodging of his former masters, Comtesse Louise and Vicomte Paul?"

"Perhaps it's by way of penance," Galapian suggested.

"Perhaps. In the meantime, you repent nothing yourself. The great problem is that of transmigration–what the ancients call metempsychosis. It's extremely simple. There's a rotation. One is here, then there. I believed that I was the Wandering Jew; I was him. But which one? For you must know that there are three principal Wandering Jews, not counting Judas and Herod's wife. Well, I was Cartaphilus, Pontius Pilate's doorman. Abbé Romorantin frequently met Isaac Laquedem, or Ahasuerus, in the Savrays' home, and it appears that it was him–I mean Laquedem–who saved the child on the night of the fire. As for the third Wandering Jew, Ozer the soldier, a villain through and through, the Abbé is seeking him on my behalf in order to stuff him, and it's for that that he gets 200 francs a month."

"He has never been madder than this!" said General Lamadou.

"There's also talk," Madame Lancelot replied, "of him becoming President of the five Academies." [37]

"Don't interrupt," cried the Doctor, "or I'll have you thrown out! Can you guess who has replaced me in the role of Cartaphilus? The Abbé has found out. He's cleverer than Monsieur Galapian! The man who has replaced me is the Man with the Long Beard at the Palais-Royal..."

"The Superb!" some exclaimed.

"Chodruc-Duclos!" others said. [38]

"Have you ever seen him sitting down? Never. And," the little Doctor added, triumphantly, "he has no cobbler, so he must mend his shoes himself, unless his soles are magic. That can happen. When I was mad, I had a pair of boots that called me Punch. One doesn't take much notice of such details. Did you know that the Prince de Polignac [39] uses the informal mode of address with Chodruc-Duclos? Oh yes! Chodruc-Duclos got down into the Prince's bedroom through the chimney last Tuesday, and said to him: 'How goes the air tax, old chap?' [40] The Prince called out but no one came. Chodruc, or rather Cartaphilus, added: 'Tee hee! By the end of the month, you'll be in the dog-pound, my old hound!' What about that!"

"What's that supposed to mean?" asked Madame Lancelot.

"It means that France, my fatherland, has a revolution hanging from the end of her nose!"

"What's that?" cried those with governmental salaries.

"Myself, I believe it," said the Doctor. "Chodruc has a lesion in the brain. That's something to inspire confidence. Long live the King of Hearts and Yvetot's independence!" [41]

Dreading an imminent political conflagration, General Lamadou put him in chains and sent him to the lock-up.

XLV. The Fall

On the evening of the July 26, in a modest third-floor room in the Rue de l'Ouest, Comtesse Louise, Abbé Romorantin, Joli-Coeur and Fanchon Honoré were all gathered together. That had not happened for a long time.

The window looked over the Luxembourg Gardens, full of strollers. The weather was warm. The Sun was setting into distant storm clouds.

There was an unaccustomed bustle in the garden. The street, ordinarily so tranquil, rendered up those mysterious and menacing echoes that no words can describe, but which are never forgotten once one has heard them. It is as if two baleful voices are permanently stuck in the memory: the voice of the storm and the voice of the revolution.

In Comtesse Louise's room, consternation was painted on every face, but they were not talking about the threats in the street.

They were talking about Colonel Comte de Savray.

Louise was supporting her head in her hands, weeping.

"Is it possible to fall as low as that?" she said.

The poor woman recalled 11 years of noble and happy good fortune. Her son Paul was 18 years old; seven years of cruel and shameful martyrdom had followed the happy times.

She had wept for the first time on the night of the fire–but since then, there had been so many tears!

Her son, the dear child, had been abandoned by his father, ruined by his father and dishonored by his father.

There was no exaggeration in the news reported by Madame Lancelot. Even Madame Lancelot did not know everything. Colonel Comte de Savray had fallen as far as it was possible to fall. It was a hideous, incredible, diabolical fall. Comte de Savray had plunged as he pleased into the utmost depths of the filthiest abyss in which our social ills swarm. He stood accused–he, an officer and a gentleman–of everything that could degrade a sword or soil a coat-of-arms.

He had lied; he had defrauded; he had stolen; he had killed.

Joli-Coeur had come to report his flight, and the invasion of his lodgings by the authorities, where the people who were searching for him had talked loudly of ball-and-chains and prison hulks.

And that pretty young woman who was weeping said again, as mad people repeat the same refrain:

"Is it possible to have been so noble and so good? Is it possible to be so infamous and so wretched?"

XLVI. Details Seen in Retrospect

"No, that is not possible," replied Comtesse Louise's rebellious heart.

And there was, indeed, something inexplicable in all this from the purely human point-of-view. All the people reunited in Comtesse Louise's room said, as the bottom of their hearts, what she said:

"No, that is not possible."

The fact was certain, but no one believed it.

The nurse, the priest and the soldier, like the woman in mourning, rejected the evidence, searching for a supernatural key to the insoluble puzzle.

"The change occurred in the space of a single day," the Comtesse went on, translating her vague thoughts as best she could. "In a single hour, a single minute! When he left me, as we arrived at the bottom of the hill on the night of the fire, my Roland was certainly himself. When he returned to sit down beside me, after braving the fire, I felt a chill in the depths of my soul. He was indifferent to the danger that our beloved Paul had been in. That horrible spectacle of the fire, which still burns my eyes, left his heart cold. When I spoke to him of the miracle that had saved our son, he shrugged his shoulders, humming I don't know what. He never even looked at the child I was clasping to my bosom, the child that we had given up for lost! And... how can I put it? His voice was still the voice that I knew, but–in the first moments, especially–there was something in it of Sir Arthur's English accent..."

"Sir Arthur himself," the Abbé put in, shaking his head, "had been a stoutly honest gentleman for a long time. I know his story. He was a regular at the Comédie Française. One evening, he went out during the performance, and then he came back... or, rather, another Sir Arthur came back to take his place in his box. This other Sir Arthur was the one you have seen: a debauché, a drunkard, a brigand!"

"So, what is the key to these puzzles?" Louise murmured.

The Abbé, Fanchon and Joli-Coeur remained silent.

Louise continued: "That night–that dreadful night– he thought of nothing but drinking, eating and sleeping. In the hotel room where we took refuge, since our house had burned down, he had supper served. At times, he spoke of things unknown to me, boasting of shameful adventures. At other times, he blasphemed so horribly that my blood turned to ice in my veins."

The Abbé and Fanchon crossed themselves. Joli-Coeur gnawed his moustache.

The noises were still rising from the street and the garden: the sad and prophetic voices that forecast popular storms.

"Perhaps, at this very hour," Joli-Coeur said, abruptly, "he is already in the body of some other honest man, of whom he will make a rogue."

"So," murmured Comtesse Louise, whose beautiful head was slumped over her bosom, "you think I am right to wear a widow's weeds? You believe that my poor husband is dead?"

In the silence that followed, footsteps were heard climbing the staircase. A handsome young man came in, sad and pale. Coldly, without smiling, he said:

"Good evening, mother."

XLVII. Mother and Son

It was Vicomte Paul, the superb child of former times: the Vicomte Paul who had built fortifications against the English. He was now fully-grown, his figure proud and graceful. He resembled his father, Colonel Comte Roland de Savray, but he was better-looking.

Blond curls clustered around his forehead. His big blue eyes expressed sadness and gallantry.

"I need to talk to you," he said, addressing himself to Joli-Coeur before he had even kissed his mother's cheeks. "Is it true that the Comte de Savray, my father, spends his nights marching back and forth in his room?"

"It's true," the hussar replied.

"Is it true that his bed is never unmade?"

"It's true," Joli-Coeur replied. "That, and all the rest. All that is said of him is true. But is it really Monsieur le Comte? That's what we don't know any longer."

Paul bowed his head and frowned. He went to his mother, who pressed him to her heart even more tenderly than usual.

"Have you something to tell me?" she murmured.

"Yes, mother."

She made a gesture. The Abbé, Fanchon and Joli-Coeur retired to the next room.

Now, we know that the Abbé had been employed by the fat little Doctor Lunat for several years, primarily to examine all the books written in every language regarding the centuries-old myth of the Wandering Jew. The Abbé, finding his audience docile, emptied his sack and spoke of extraordinary curiosities, mainly on the subject of the Pharisee Nathan, who leased the Temple to merchants.[42]

This Pharisee is the fourth Wandering Jew, and 60 times a millionaire.

The fifth is the valet of Caiaphas.

Vicomte Paul, meanwhile, sat down on a stool at his mother's feet. He put his blond head on Comtesse Louise's knees. She could read his big blue eyes like a book.

"You're in pain?" she said.

"Not when I'm here, close to you, mother dear," he replied, while a nascent smile appeared on his lips.

XLVIII. The Confession

She leaned over to place a long kiss on a forehead as soft of that of a young woman.

"Mother," said Paul, "if I did not love you so much, I would die. I am always alone. I shun those of my age so as not to hear what they are saying, for they often speak ill of him whose name you bear, and whom I call my father. The poor friends who remain faithful to us try hard to console me with strange fables and children's tales, but I am not a child, mother, and I no longer believe what I don't understand."

"That's true," murmured Comtesse Louise. "You're a savant now, my dear Paul. You are much more of a savant than Abbé Romorantin, who still believes in my former happiness, in the affection and the generosity of Comte Roland de Savray, my beloved husband... oh, if you could only remember...!"

"I remember only too well!" Paul murmured, with a sort of groan.

The Comtesse did not hear him, and continued: "If you knew, as I do, what a heart your father had! How much delicacy, and beautiful pride! What love! What honor...!"

"I believe that, mother," Vicomte Paul put in, his eyes moist with tears. "I believe that as I believe in God!"

"What is it, then, that you don't believe, my dear?" Comtesse Louise asked.

Paul remained silent for a moment; then he covered his face with his hands.

"There are two things that are impossible!" he murmured, eventually, in a discouraged tone. "It would be necessary also to believe in Bluebeard, in the Bogeyman, in the Ogre, in Hop o'my Thumb... although there are many examples, mother, many established examples of men of good character, loyal, even chivalrous, who suddenly fell into the utmost depths of the abyss of evil!"

"Child," said the Comtesse, with gentle firmness, "if I am mistaken, allow me my error. I would dearly like to die, but that must not be your fate!"

Paul knelt down, covering Comtesse Louise's cold hands with kisses.

"Oh, mother, mother!" he went on, in a voice tremulous with held-back tears, "I will believe in anything that you wish... but you have extracted a promise from me never to risk my life in a duel, because it is yours..."

"Because it is God's," the poor mother corrected him.

"Someone has insulted me..."

"Already!"

"Release me from my promise, mother!"

XLIX. The Vision

Comtesse Louise looked at him with a mother's love, full of dread and courage.

"Someone has insulted you?" she repeated. "And who has dared to insult you?"

A vivid blush replaced Vicomte Paul's pallor

"As I came out of the Collège," he said, his voice becoming lower in spite of himself, "I heard, as usual, the cruel mockery of the three or four wretches who follow me: the son of the General who was second-in-command at Tours; the son of the former Prefect of Tours; the son of Madame Lancelot, from Tours. The other pupils liked me before; those three have created the void around me, as if I were a leper. Have we done them any harm, mother?"

"Never, my poor child. But their parents have seen us so happy!"

"According to my habit, in order to escape their sarcasm, I went into the church of Saint-Etienne-du-Mont. I often go there. I like to pray to good Sainte Genevieve. I beg her to send us the one who has already protected us twice. I was kneeling by the aisle on the left-hand side. I wasn't praying, for I had too much anger in my heart. I saw the rays of the setting Sun filtering through the holes in the rood-screen to inundate the crucifix above the main altar with colored light. The unhappy man who annoyed Our Lord has been repentant for 1,800 years, mother. He who is Forgiveness must have forgiven him. I said to myself: 'His ordeal must be over; we shall not see him again.'

145

"Suddenly, by the light of the candles burning next to the reliquary, I noticed a young woman kneeling. I looked at her without knowing whence came the profound emotion that made my heart beat faster. She stood up. I was dazzled, as if by the sight of an angel.

"Oh, mother, she was so beautiful! And it was as if her smile could appease celestial anger! I threw myself towards her, for I had recognized her..."

"You knew her?" exclaimed the Comtesse.

"Listen!" murmured Vicomte Paul. "A little while ago, I lied when I said I no longer believe what I don't understand. I believe all of it, mother, and I very often dream of her..."

"Her? Who are you talking about?"

"I'm talking," Vicomte Paul replied. "I'm talking of... Is it really necessary to say her name? Perhaps you no longer know it, but for my own part, I have never forgotten the sweet and pale face of the one who shared the days of my childhood..."

"Lotte!" Louise put in, prey to a sudden anxiety. "The daughter of the..."

She stopped, but Vicomte Paul finished for her:

"*The daughter of the Wandering Jew*. I've seen her again, mother!"

L. *The* Marseillaise

In the next room, the good Abbé Romorantin was talking to Fanchon and Joli-Coeur.

"One can find anything in books. Doctor Lunat is as mad as a March hare, but his madness has permitted me to do wonderful research. The hand of Providence is in it. Every day, I learn something new. My friends, there is nothing astonishing in encountering the Wandering Jew three days running in Paris. Bertola, cited by Matthew Paris, affirms that the Eternal Traveler has the ability to remain in any place where there is pestilence, famine or war. That counts, for him, as a forced march."

"In Paris, thank God," Fanchon the nurse objected, "we have neither pestilence, nor war, nor famine."

A song was audible in the Rue de l'Ouest. No one took any notice of it at first.

"When he is encountered three days running in Paris," the Abbé pronounced, peremptorily, "it is because he has the right to remain there. Bertola is precise: it is because Paris has famine, pestilence or..."

"Listen!" Joli-Coeur interrupted.

The song became more distinct. There were metallic and vibrant notes that stirred the soul and impregnated it with fear.

The old hussar's eyes caught fire. "I know that tune!" he said. "It's the *Marseillaise*! Monsieur l'Abbé is right! It's possible that we have neither pestilence not famine in Paris, but when they sing the *Marseillaise*, by jingo, we've got war... and civil war, at that! Very well, I'm in it!"

LI. The Insult

On the other side of the partition-wall, Vicomte Paul, at his mother's knees, went on:

"It only needed the blink of an eye for me to recognize her.

"It was Lotte's gentle face on the body of an adorable young woman. My entire heart went out to her. I wanted to follow her, but she slipped along the right-hand aisle like a ghost, and I heard no footsteps on the pavement. The church door closed behind her. It had seemed to me that, at the moment when she took the holy water, her angelic smile was searching for me.

"I went out in my turn.

"You know, mother, that the one who refused hospitality to our Savior does not have the right to go into a church. Undoubtedly, he had waited for her at the foot of the steps. I saw a man of tall stature who was moving away, hand in hand with a little girl..."

"A little girl?" Comtesse Louise repeated.

"Yes," Vicomte Paul replied, hesitantly. "I'm telling you this as if it were a dream. The beautiful young person had disappeared, replaced by Lotte as she was... my dear little Lotte... and her body so frail, so graceful, had the transparency of old...

"Alas," the young man went on, his smile turning to a frown, "my enemies had waited for me in the forecourt. When they saw me, there was a chorus of jeers.

" 'His father is disgraced!' cried Roger, the son of the Brigade Commander.

" 'He'll be cashiered!' added the Prefect's son.

148

" 'He has cheated at cards,' said the Lancelot boy. 'He's a deserter, a thief, a murderer!'

"The Man was already far away, but he turned around without pausing. I pressed both hands to my heart, and I went to pass between my insulters without raising my head–for I was thinking of my promise and of you, mother–when Roger said:

" 'Go on, coward, go tell the good news to the god-daughter of King Louis XVIII!'

"At that moment, Lotte turned around in her turn. She had heard.

" 'You are a liar and a coward!' I cried.

"And my hand struck Roger's cheek twice, because he was the closest to me."

LII. The Forecourt of Notre-Dame

You might have taken Comtesse Louise for a marble statue, so white was her face. She tried to speak, but Vicomte Paul closed her mouth, saying:

"I haven't finished, Mother. I went away slowly, accompanied by their threats. I wanted to follow Lotte and her father, not because I thought I might discover their address, in the ordinary sense of the word–for the one of whom we are speaking can have no dwelling-place–but because I wanted to keep Lotte in sight for as long as possible.

"Besides, my head was on fire. It was necessary for me to recover my balance before presenting myself to you.

"Lotte and the Wandering Jew went down the Rue Saint-Jacques as far as the Seine. They went over the bridge. They both went into a large old house behind Notre-Dame: the next-to-the-last in the Rue du Cloître.

"I waited. I never saw them come out.

"Night was falling, and I began to have doubts. Was it believable that the Man whose penitence had lasted 1,800 years could reside under a roof?

"I began to make my way back here. At the moment when I left the forecourt, I turned round to glance in the direction of the great facade of Notre-Dame.

"The last glimmer of twilight illuminated the balcony that joins the two square towers. I saw–or thought I saw–the Man who had not the right to pause passing back and forth behind the colonnettes...

"All around me in the street, somber groups formed. Under the workmen's blouses, as under the coats of bourgeois gentlefolk, the glint of weapons could be seen. And there were threatening voices saying: 'This is the night! Up with the charter, down with the charioteer!' "

LIII. Eavesdropping

After the evening meal, Vicomte Paul kissed his mother even more tenderly than usual, and wished her good night. The Comtesse, sad but apparently calm, went back into her apartment.

As he left, Vicomte Paul said:

"Poor mother! She doesn't know!"

He was mistaken; mothers know everything.

In Vicomte Paul's room, the old hussar Joli-Coeur was waiting for him. As he came in, Paul said to him:

"Old man, do you know where I can obtain a pair of dueling-pistols and two good swords?"

Joli-Coeur looked at him, utterly astounded.

"I'm fighting tomorrow," Vicomte Paul added, trying to smile.

At that moment, bare feet crept noiselessly into the corridor, and Comtesse Louise, shivering from top to toe, put her ear to the keyhole.

"Who are you fighting?" Joli-Coeur asked.

"Roger, the son of the brigade commander at Tours."

"Ah!" said the old hussar. "His wife was very fearful at one time that Monsieur le Comte would not be promoted to General. The family's not top drawer, though military." After a pause, he added: "And why are you fighting Monsieur Roger?"

"Because he insulted my mother."

Comtesse Louise was obliged to support herself against the corridor wall. Her legs were giving way beneath her.

"That's a reason, all right," said Joli-Coeur. "And where are you fighting?"

"Behind the Montparnasse Cemetery."

"I know the place. It's a good spot."

The Comtesse's hands were clutching at her heart.

"Do you have seconds?" Joli-Coeur continued his interrogation.

"No," Vicomte Paul replied. "If you bring one of your comrades, that will make two."

Refuse, wretch, refuse! thought Comtesse Louise. *It's your duty! Save your master's son.*

But Joli-Coeur was only a soldier. He said:

"That's right. With me, that makes two."

Comtesse Louise felt an indescribable anguish in her heart then. She had nothing in the world but the treasure she idolized: her son, her Paul, her soul!

Imagine how she was menaced by this supreme agony: to lose her only son. She saw the grey extent of the long high wall of the cemetery. She saw the dismal setting at the hour preceding the rising of the Sun. She saw the sinister gleam of swords; men coldly loading pistols, measuring out their paces and clapping their stony hands three times.

The powder caught fire.

There was a scream.

And a poor young voice calling: "Mother...!"

Then, a stretcher with a corpse, its contours outlined beneath a linen sheet.

Under the sheet, a child with a red wound beneath his breast.

She saw that. She slid to her knees, kissing the ground that was moistened by tears, and stammered:

"My God! My God! My God! Have pity!"

At that very moment, Vicomte Paul was saying to Joli-Coeur:

"It's settled, then: you'll come to awaken me tomorrow morning at 4 a.m., and we'll go."

LIV. A Night in Paris

The sky was a profound blue: the innumerable stars had none of the scintillant brilliance of a stormy night. It was warm, but a gentle breeze was soughing in the foliage of the Luxembourg. The Milky Way spanned the firmament with its indistinct and misty diagonal.

The city was not asleep, and yet there was a vast silence. Not a carriage-wheel was rolling on the mute high road.

When the voice of the bustling city chances to fall silent, when the dull rotation of wheels and the hoof beats of horses suddenly ceases, the Parisian night is afraid.

The door of Comtesse Louise's apartment-house opened softly. Midnight chimed on the clock of the Luxembourg Palace. A woman, enveloped in a dark mantle, came out and went down the Rue de l'Ouest with an unsteady gait. A large black-clad company was stationed at the corner of the Rue de Vaugirard, seemingly motionless and mute. The crowd parted to let the woman pass.

Comtesse Louise could see that there were men armed with iron bars in the heart of the company, silently prising up paving-stones.

Five hundred paces further on, a detachment of the Royal Guard had taken up a position near the Rue du Pot-de-Fer-Saint-Sulpice. The soldiers were playing cards around a fire. The officers were strolling around, chatting about the taking of Algiers, news of which had just broken.

Officers and soldiers alike were joking about Parisians who wanted to play the game of barricades.

When Comtesse Louise passed in front of the galleries of the Odéon, the breeze carried a distant ringing sound to her ears. The people nearby said: "That's the tocsin!"

Cheerful students spilled out of the Café Tabourcy and cried: "Long live the charter!"

Revolutions always wish long life in this manner to the things they want to bury.

These students were handsome young men. The sight of them made Comtesse Louise press on, thinking of her son.

A barricade was already being raised in the Rue Racine. The new streets are good for that; the roadway is nicely raised. At the windows, students were amusing themselves watching the work.

The black gables of the Rue des Mathurins-Saint-Jacques and the Hôtel de Cluny were sharply outlined against the sky, speaking of the Christian times when the cathedrals were erected, while an atheist professor, perched on a boundary-marker, offered a course in free thought. These professors are like snarling dogs, save for the respect that one must pay them. To prevent them barking, it is only necessary to throw them a bone–but if one leaves them with empty jaws, they bite–and their bite is rabid.

All along the Rue Saint-Jacques paving-stones were being taken up, and to the sound of laughter.

There were urchins who said, as they erected barricades: "Mummy will really tell me off!"

Comtesse Louise arrived at the Petit-Pont, guarded at one end by men in blouses and at the other by dragoons. Those which were defending the heritage of Saint

Louis were here, those who were playing the blind man's bluff of Revolution were there; between them ran the patient Seine, always the same. The two sides of the river were Paris. Each camp called out gaily to the other while waiting for the battle to start.

LV. The Forecourt of Notre-Dame (2)

When Comtesse Louise arrived at the forecourt of Notre-Dame, she was very tired and out of breath. Instinctively, she raised her eyes towards the marvelous walkway connecting the two towers. The frail colonnettes stood out vaguely in the darkness, but there was no human movement there.

The forecourt itself was utterly deserted. In the midst of the fever that had taken hold of the awakened city, the immense church seemed to be a sleeping sentinel. Next to it was that other immensity, respectable but lugubrious symbol of administrative charity, the Hôtel-Dieu–a menacing sphinx lying across that cheerful riverbank, two steps from the cathedral, within easy reach of Charlemagne's palace, silently posing to priests and kings the riddle of the misery that gives birth to Revolutions. Not by itself–for, since the world began, patient misery has lain down to die without ever rebelling–but through the tribunes who have calculated what they might gain in power, prestige and money by serving misery as an artillery to reduce the almshouses to rubble.

The universe is growing old. It is said that the seasons are becoming confused. The Moon, visibly deteriorated, donates its disquiet to the Observatory. But God is not old.

High up, at the very top of the ancient cathedral, there was a man who was contemplating the mad city, engaged in hunting down an old King for the profit of another old man who wanted to be King.

This man had been walking for 18 centuries, knee-deep in human insanity. He knew what misery earns from the bloody pleadings of its advocates. He was deep in thought.

And, a melancholy reflection of the world that does not know how to pause, the Wandering Jew–having completed his circuit–was forced to come down again.

Children laugh as they watch a fussy squirrel turning a wheel in which it is encaged. They say that the squirrel is working.

For 1,800 years that Jew had watched the rotating cage in which humanity works, without laughing.

LVI. The Equerry's House

Comtesse Louise went towards the house that his son had mentioned: the next-to-the-last in the Rue du Cloître-Notre-Dame. It was a grandiose dwelling, retaining an impression of aristocratic domination among the bourgeois homes that surrounded it. It was called the Equerry's House because, in the days of the three royal sons of Catherine de Medici, it had belonged to the noble Equerry Marie Minot, Seigneur of Blay-le-Fossé, Master of the Halberdiers of the Paris Chapter.[43]

Comtesse Louise came to a halt in front of the massive door, but did not dare raise the knocker. She crossed to the other side of the street in order to study the windows, which were all closed and shuttered, from the top floor to the bottom. A large placard hung above the door. Comtesse Louise could read, by the light of nearby street-lamp, *Demolition Produce For Sale*.

It occurred to Comtesse Louise that her son must have been mistaken, for this was a condemned house already abandoned by its inhabitants. She went back to the door and pushed it. The door opened, no longer having any lock or latch. Comtesse Louise went into a spacious courtyard, where various debris was untidily heaped up. The door closed behind her.

A strange chill ran through the Comtesse's veins as she looked around with child-like terror. There was nothing there but silence and immobility.

The courtyard was surrounded by a sort of cloister, pierced by three high-arched openings. If the Comtesse had taken heed of her fright, she would have withdrawn

160

immediately, but her mother's heart remained superior to all terrors.

I am here for my son's sake, she told herself.

And she selected one of the three arches at random.

It was the one to her right. It led to a vestibule where a vast stone staircase reached its foot. It no longer had its banisters, which were heaped up in the courtyard with the other items for sale.

The Comtesse went up.

From the first floor, she saw that the windows lacked frames and that all the doors had been taken out; they, too, were in piles in the courtyard.

She went into the first room she came to, large and high-ceilinged, then another, equally bare. All the doorways of these abandoned rooms opened into a wide corridor. Comtesse Louise counted a dozen rooms. She went into each of them in turn, impelled by some mysterious hope; all of them were equally deserted.

After the twelfth, there was nothing further on the corridor. Through a frameless window, she saw that she had completed the circuit of the house.

Discouraged, she was thinking about going down when it seemed to her that she heard a noise at the far end of the corridor. In the darkness, a pale form was visible: the shadow of a child, which slipped away and disappeared.

"Lotte!" called Comtesse Louise.

The echoes along the corridor repeated he name: *Lotte*!

The silence fell again, more sinister than before.

Suddenly, on the floor above, a slow and regular step, like the noise produced by a clock's pendulum, resonated on the tiles of the corridor.

Comtesse Louise listened intently, recovering her breath.

The noise became more distant, dying away.

A man had passed by immediately above her head

Comtesse Louise threw herself forward and climbed the unguarded staircase at a run. By the time she had reached the upper corridor, the noise of footsteps had ceased, but again she saw that white and indecisive form at its end–its furthest end.

She called out as before:

"Lotte! Lotte!"

There was the same echo–and the same silence.

Comtesse Louise went into a dozen rooms in succession, empty and bare.

As she came out of the twelfth, the man's footsteps, slow and regular, passed above her head. She climbed up with all the speed that her weary and trembling legs could muster.

There was no one in the third-floor corridor! There was no one in the rooms–only, as she left the twelfth, the little shadow gliding along the gallery, at its end, its furthest end.

"Lotte! Lotte! My darling Lotte!"

The echo–then the silence.

Then, the sound of footsteps, slow and regular–but this time, on the floor below.

Comtesse Louise went back down. It was like one of those exhausting dreams in which one is in feverish pursuit of something unattainable.

For hours, Comtesse Louise climbed up and came back down, running after the impossible.

She felt broken by exhaustion and by terror; the cold reached into the marrow of her bones, but she went on and on, because a distant voice in the depths of her being was speaking the name of her beloved son.

The grey gleams of morning entered by the large windows that opened on to the courtyard. The Hôtel-Dieu clock chimed three in the morning.

LVII. Vicomte Paul's Awakening

At that moment, Joli-Coeur knocked on Vicomte Paul's door.[44] Paul leapt out of bed, saying:

"Hush! No noise! Make sure we don't wake my mother!"

Joli-Coeur had swords, pistols and a companion, a hussar like himself. Within the blink of an eye, Vicomte Paul was dressed. With his seconds, he climbed into a fiacre that was waiting for them in the street.

As he passed his mother's room, Vicomte Paul, his eyes misted and his heart constricted, said to himself: *If she remains alone...!*

A duel is a party to two crimes: a suicide and an assassination.

Every man despises it in the depths of his heart, but it will live as long as the world, because it is the product of three immoralities: hatred, stupidity and pride.

And because men, brave in the face of the blade, become as timid as chickens when that imbecile phantom precedent shows them its teeth.[45]

LVIII. The Third Hour

As the third chime sounded on the Hôtel-Dieu clock, a noise was audible in the courtyard of the Equerry's House. Comtesse Louise looked out of the window and saw a man of tall stature, who was opening the latchless door, after having crossed the courtyard.

She called out, but her voice was drowned out by the noise of the door falling shut.

Her knees folded beneath her. Two arms held her up and prevented her from collapsing on the cold tiles. A beautiful young woman was there, bending over her.

"Lotte! Is that you? How you have grown!" murmured Comtesse Louise.

But the thought of her son could never let her rest. "Have pity on me!" she added. "Lift me up! We must run! I want to tell him what I know. I have no other hope but you. Paul is going to fight a duel..."

She felt the young woman's arms shiver beneath her own.

"Come," said the young woman. "Father has not forbidden me to follow him."

"Do you know, then, where the duel is taking place?"

"Father knows everything," Lotte replied. "He's going to a place behind the Montparnasse Cemetery."

"That's it!"

"Come on! Father will be there before us."

LIX. The Duel

For the moment, Paris was asleep. The government's soldiers slept in their bivouacs or their guardhouses; the insurrection's soldiers lay down behind their half-erected barricades. Only the sentinels kept their eyes open.

Comtesse Louise, leaning on the arm of the handsome fully-grown woman who had Lotte's face, retraced her steps along the route she had already traveled once that night. They crossed the Petit-Pont and went back up the Rue Saint-Jacques–but instead of turning towards the Rue de l'Ouest, Louise de Savray and her companion turned left at the Luxembourg, heading for the southern boulevards.

Behind the Montparnasse Cemetery there was then a vast and dusty plain, where a few factories were under construction. This plain had the uniquely desolate ugliness of land that has already ceased to be fields but which is not yet part of the city.

About 500 paces from the Cemetery, there was an enclosure, confined by a brand-new wooden trellis, containing patchy lucerne. It might have been an acre and a half in extent, and the owner had taken care to place a pole bearing the inscribed notice that is the ultimate in Parisian grotesquerie: *Hunting Rights Reserved.*

It was to this spot that Vicomte Paul, assisted by his two dragoons, had come to meet Roger and his two comrades, the heir of the former Prefect of Tours and the son of Madame Lancelot.

Roger was the insulted party. He chose the sword, with which he was an expert.

166

They went into the enclosure, despite the notice, and the adversaries took up their positions on suitable ground.

They took off their coats. The combat began immediately, and from the first passes Vicomte Paul had blood on his shirt.

The daylight was already bright, and the Sun was rising behind the dome of the Val-de-Grâce.[46]

Suddenly, a loud cry resounded from the corner of the Cemetery. There were two women there, one of whom fell fainting into the other's arms.

Paul's sword became unsteady in his hand, in spite of his intention. He had recognized his mother's voice.

Roger, profiting from his advantage, lunged before the seconds could interpose themselves. Vicomte Paul fell, but not before his enemy's steel.

His mother's cry had rent his heart.

Roger's sword-thrust had been intercepted by the body of a man of tall stature, who had appeared quite unexpectedly between the two adversaries. One might have thought that he had sprung out of the ground.

As it touched the body of this man, Roger's blade shattered like a dry straw, and its chaff was scattered far and wide on the ground.

LX. The Prophecy

"Gentlemen," said the stranger to Roger and his two seconds, "those who wish to fight can indulge themselves today to their heart's content. Listen!"

He extended an arm towards Paris, from which the noise of rifle-fire was already audible.

"Your fathers," the stranger went on, "are in the service of the King who still sits upon his throne. They must be embarrassed, not knowing whether to support or betray him. Go save them the trouble. The King will be defeated: they may turn their backs on him."

One cannot deny that a great many venerable citizens would be delighted to encounter a prophet of this kind in the first hour of a revolution. It would save a great deal of groping and calm a great many anxieties.

For if, in the end, all things considered, the insurrection is put down...

Of course, of course, but if the revolution is successful...

Damn it! In these cases, an honest man who wants to keep his position finds himself in the most annoying perplexity!

The fiacre that had brought Vicomte Paul took him back to the lodgings in the Rue de l'Ouest, accompanied by Comtesse Louise and the beautiful young woman. The two women sat down at the bedside of the feverish unfortunate.

Fanchon the nurse wept with joy at seeing Lotte again and crossed herself, saying:

"If God wishes it, the house will be filled with good fortune again!"

LXI. An Essay on Revolutions

Monsieur Galapian was often accused of having spent the Revolution of July 1830 in the depths of a cellar. Such mistakes are easily believable, and in 15 or 20 centuries, a rascal's name can spring up like a mushroom in the middle of the garden of history. Historical terrain is a bed uniquely favorable to such fungi. No one makes revolutions. They are crises that arise spontaneously, when the National Guard gets bored.

Our subject, however, soars far above politics, so we must keep such frivolities for later.

The editor of a newspaper dear to the Academy had written, from the depths of his armchair–so nicely portrayed by Monsieur Ingres [47]–and during an attack of gout: "Unfortunate King! Unfortunate France!" The words caused a furor. The unfortunate France hunted down the unfortunate King–a first-rate hunter, fervent Christian and loyal gentleman–to put in his place a more fortunate King, a skillful fisherman and convinced bourgeois who scarcely troubled himself with Mass. Who was surprised? The editor of the newspaper, when his gout had passed.

Except that, to accomplish this "exchange partners," people were cutting one another's throats in the streets for three days with marvelous vigor. That is the comic element of the drama. On this point alone, the editor of the newspaper is serious–but not quite as serious as the Sire de Framboisy.[48]

Eighteen years later, another newspaper became the hunter of the bourgeois King, who was not a wicked man, although he had done wicked things in the course of his life. Again, there was much blood and ruination.

Now, there is no longer a King, but there are still newspapers, and republics hunt one another. Half of Paris occasionally jumps to attention, and the newspapers enjoy themselves.

And the people? Oh well, they earn a living by demolishing and rebuilding Paris on command.

LXII. At the Three Kings

In the Rue Pierre-Lescot, on the site now occupied by the Hôtel du Louvre–the banal palace that accommodates every prince and commercial traveler in the world–there was a poor, cramped and sordid five-story house that did not enjoy a good reputation. It was called the House of Jews, even though its sign depicted the black heads of the three royal magi.

On the fifth floor of this house lived Chodruc-Duclos, that strange person known under the Restoration and in the early years of Louis Philippe's reign as "the Superb" or "the Man with the Long Beard." No one remembers those names nowadays. *Sic transit gloria.*[49]

On the fourth floor dwelt a woman of enormous corpulence, named Madame Potiphar.[50] She hired out rooms for the night. Her lodgers included the Pharisee Nathan, Caiaphas' valet and others.

On the third, there was a mysterious individual who could be heard moving about all night, and whose bed was never disturbed.

One the second, there was a second-hand dealer called Holofernes,[51] whom the police kept under paternal surveillance.

Finally, on the first and ground floors, a tavern of the lowest rank opened its squalid rooms and its redoubtable private rooms.

In spite of the scholarly research of Doctor Lunat, Member of the Institute, no one has ever been able to discover whether the persons assembled for a drunken feast at the tavern in the Rue Pierre-Lescot, in the House of Jews, on the night of July 28 and 29, 1830, were

171

princes in disguise or mere tramps. What might incline one to the former opinion was the presence of an exceedingly beautiful woman with a German accent, heavily laden with fake diamonds, who drank enormous quantities of kirschwasser, answered to the name of Herodias and appeared to be intimately acquainted with the Colonel Comte de Savray, a filthy bandit who reeked of wine and tobacco.

The reader must forgive us these details, for which we humbly beg the pardon of our female readers. They are absolutely necessary to our story, which is much more serious than it seems, and can only maintain its high character and strict truthfulness.

From words spoken in the course of the drunken orgy, an educated man skilled in the art of deduction would have been able to infer that the haggard women surrounding the table amply laden with cheap wine included Lot's daughter, Barabbas' niece and several other illustrious ladies.[52] Among the male guests, the three brothers, Korah, Dathan and Abiram distinguished themselves with their witty remarks.[53] The lodger Holofernes also seemed to be a pleasant companion, but no one could equal the liveliness of Cartaphilus, Pontius Pilate's doorkeeper, who preferred to be known here by the nickname Chodruc-Duclos.

All these people seemed to be rendering homage to the Colonel Comte de Savray, who was the King of the revels, and who was universally addressed as Ozer.

Ozer wore an old hussar's uniform that was disgraceful to look upon, but he was the best-dressed of the entire assembly.

"Did you know," he said, deftly filling his beer-glass with brandy, "that the old blunderer Ahasuerus is in Paris?"

"Isaac Laquedem!" they cried. "That nothing!"

"An apostate!"

"A false brother!"

"A wretch who took it into his head to repent!"

"He's setting himself up," the Colonel went on, "to afford his worthy protection to my wife and son–I mean the wife and son of the idiot fencing-master to whom I did the honor of appropriating his skin."

"That Comtesse Louise is certainly the most tiresome of all bigots!"

"And that Vicomte Paul is a young simpleton who shows every evidence of wanting to work like an honest man!"

The Colonel swallowed a magnificent draught. "Paris will dance tomorrow!" he said. "I propose that the friendly society should play a trick on that sleeping dog Ahasuerus. We'll go to the barricades. He'll be there, I'm sure, under the pretext of saving someone or playing the hypocrite. We'll all go at him together and do away with him."

There was frantic applause.

Lot's daughter, however–who had the age and the experience–objected:

"Isaac Laquedem is invulnerable, so they say." In support of which she sang, in a basso-profundo voice:

> "*I've seen in Europe,*
> "*Just as in Asia,*
> "*Battles and conflicts*
> "*That cost many lives:*
> "*I've passed through them all*
> "*Without a single wound!*"

"Chocs doesn't rhyme with Europe,"[54] observed Chodruc-Duclos, not without a certain scorn.

The Colonel restored silence with a gesture.

"During the time I was Sir Arthur," he said, "I heard a good story told by that madman Doctor Lunat, who studies us all with such passion. He's the sanest man in the Academy. Doctor Lunat told the tale of a pocket with a hole, from which five *sous* fell out and fell out again, incessantly. If we could bind Isaac Laquedem's hands, put a hole in his waistcoat pocket, and whip him around the world a couple of times with a riding-crop, can you imagine the tidy sum we might amass?"

"We'd have to get hold of him first..."

"Tomorrow, we'll hunt him all over Paris!"

At that moment, Herodias put her hand on Colonel de Savray's shoulder, and said:

"Look at the clock, Ozer my dear."

Ozer obeyed. The clock's hands stood at five minutes to midnight.

Immediately, Ozer–or Colonel de Savray, as others might call him–got up, threw his napkin down and vanished, followed by Queen Herodias.

Around the table, the guests exchanged suggestive winks.

"The hour has come!" said Holofernes.

Chodruc-Duclos added: "All the way! [55] It seems that at this particular moment, a three-year-old might kill him!"

LXIII. Herod's Soldier's Hour

Bertola says nothing about this subject, and that is a mistake. Herzélius seems to have completely ignored the subject. Matthew Paris himself, so reliable in his way, is as mute as a fish.[56] We have nothing to go on but a text by Schedt, brought to light by Doctor Lunat.

Schedt gives us to understand, in three rather confused lines that are to be found in volume XXIII of his *Legendry*, that every day, at midnight, the execrable soldier Ozer–who extended the vinegar-soaked sponge– shuts himself up in his room with a casket that he clenches in his arms.

For 30 minutes or so, he lies as if dead, guarded by Herod's wife, who has his full confidence.

Schedt says nothing about the contents of the casket. He was mad, according to Doctor Lunat–on whose behalf the good Abbé Romorantin had paid a great deal of money for an unpublished century [57] by Michel de Notre-Dame, relating to the immortal days of July, which certainly mentions the casket (in veiled terminology) but swears (mysteriously) that there was nothing inside it.

LXIV. The Invitation

After three-quarters of an hour, the infamous Ozer, still occupying the usurped body of Colonel Comte Roland de Savray, and Queen Herodias came back into the banqueting hall. Ozer was slightly pale, but a large glass of brandy soon brought the glow back to his cheeks.

The orgy went on, wilder than before.

Some time after daybreak, Ozer said:

"Comrades, I've never kept a body as long as that of Colonel Roland de Savray. It's a handsome and sound body, in which I've enjoyed myself enormously, but it's burnt out. This booby of a Colonel is accused of forgery, theft, treason and I don't know what else. The world still doesn't admit our jolly pleasantries. It must go. In the meantime, I'm telling you that I'll be letting go of the Colonel's body, which might as well go to the galleys. I've a fancy to be some kind of Minister in the new government, or the son of the new King; it'll make a change for me, and it'll do wonders for us! At 2 a.m., tomorrow night, I invite you to my 188th birthday. There'll be truffles all round!"

In the midst of the acclamation that followed this remarkable speech, a volley of musket-fire was heard close by, in the Place du Palais-Royal.

Everyone got up excitedly.

The volley was followed by a few isolated shots.

"To the barricades! To the barricades!" was the cry from every quarter.

"God damn it!" said Chodruc-Duclos. "Here's something to give my old mate Prince de Polignac a good laugh! So, tee hee! The *carmagnole*'s on! [58] Let's go get our own back on the slow coaches who didn't want to make us Prefect!"

LXV. The July Sun

Oh, when the sultry Sun warmed the great
*   flagstones*
Of bridges and our deserted quays,
When the bells were howling and the hail
*   of bullets*
Whistled and rained from the air...

Poets follow in the cannons' train, singing thus–some in magnificent verse, like Auguste Barbier,[59] others...

Casimir Delavigne [60] wrote the *Parisienne*–but Paris, which is not so very particular, becomes mad with joy when it is sung. Paris made a success of the *Parisienne*.

The July Sun acquired a circumstantial celebrity– although, to be fair, Paris took 15 full days before making fun of the July Sun of the *Parisienne* and the new King's umbrella.

It was there, the July Sun, playing on the ventilation-shaft of the cellar where Monsieur Galapian and a few other Men of State listened to history passing by. It hurled its morning upon a murderous scene. By the fair light of its caresses, thousands of valiant birdbrains killed one another without knowing why. Some cried "Up with this!" and others cried "Up with that!" and the rifles spoke and the cannons thundered, and *the bells were howling*, as the poem says...

About 10 a.m., three men came down the Rue Saint-Jacques, where the battle was raging conscientiously. One of these men had no weapon save for a long staff; the other two had sabers in their hands. They wore workmen's blouses over their hussars' uniforms. These latter two were our friend Joli-Coeur and his companion, Vicomte Paul's other second. They were trying to get back to their barracks, situated in the Rue de Reuilly, off the Faubourg Saint-Antoine. To do that, they had to cross the city in revolt.

The man with the staff had not said where he was bound, but having chosen his path, he seemed to take a few shots that were not aimed at him, and lifted up the wounded.

At the head of the Petit-Pont, there was a superb barricade defended by students and workers. The Professor who had earlier been preaching from a boundary-marker had gone home, on the grounds that shots were not arguments. He had promised himself that he would come back after the battle.

Students and workers surrounded our three men. The hussars' blouses were lifted up.

"We're conscripts," said Joli-Coeur, "who've probably been thinking about it longer than you. We've charged in our time to the sound of the *Marseillaise* and are, in consequence, no strangers to the tricolor. But the uniform is the uniform, and there's something that appeals to a soldier's honor. Either let us pass or break our heads properly–it's your choice, youngsters!"

The insurgents' ranks opened, while their leader–a polytechnic student–said: "Go on, old moustaches; you'll be ours tomorrow!"

This was no lie; that is what diminishes the admiration of many men for military honor. It is true that if power shifts, the fatherland remains, albeit sorely wounded.

Joli-Coeur and his comrade clambered over the piled-up paving-stones. Only the man with the long staff remained on the other side of the barricade.

At that moment, a troop approached along the Quai Saint-Michel. Those composing it had the appearance of authentic bandits; they were the guests at the House of Jews in the Rue Pierre-Lescot.

Their leader cried out:

"Finally, there he is! Someone get hold of him and someone else shoot him!"

LXVI. Torment

The leader of the band was pointing at the man with the long staff, who was staring at him fixedly in his turn. They seemed to know one another. One might have thought that the Man had stayed inside the barricade for the express purpose of awaiting the bandit chief.

However, the workers and the students commanded by the student of the Ecole Polytechnique were not men to commit an assassination, or to allow one to be committed. The newcomers' appearance was against them, although their officer wore an old cavalry Colonel's uniform and he shouted out his name: the Comte de Savray. He was about to be ordered to keep clear, when the barricade was attacked from the front by a company of the line and from the flank by a detachment of gendarmes coming down the Quai de la Tournelle. There was a moment of utter confusion, during which the Colonel Comte de Savray and his band laid hands on the man with the staff.

He, moreover, offered no resistance at all.

He allowed himself to be bound and carried off to the Quai Saint-Michel, which was completely deserted.

As it is the story of the Wandering Jew that we are telling, and not that of the July Revolution, we shall leave the barricade to follow Isaac Laquedem, fallen thus into the power of his deadliest enemies.

Ozer and his myrmidons stopped in the middle of the Quai Saint-Michel, between a useless barricade begun by overzealous constructors and an overturned milk-cart. They were only visible from windows and the other bank of the river–but all the windows were shut, and the other bank was fully occupied with its own affairs.

As soon as they had arrived at this favorable spot, the false Comte de Savray brought his sword down heavily upon Isaac's head. Barabbas threw him to the ground, handling him like a brigand, and the three sacrilegious levites, Korah, Dathan and Abiram, trampled him underfoot, while the Pharisee spat in his face.

Herodias was there to watch over Ozer. She always carried a flask of prussic acid in her pocket, as if it were an item of toiletry.

Herodias came up to the stricken Isaac, unstoppered her flask and poured its entire contents over the Wandering Jew's face.

"Be careful of your hand!" he said to her.

A few drops of the burning liquid had indeed fallen on to the hands of Herodias, who began emitting howls of pain.

Isaac smiled. The corrosive liquid ran into his eyes and between his lips. As it was caught by the hairs of his moustache, he licked them, saying: "I'm thirsty!"

Five pistol-barrels were simultaneously applied to his forehead. They discharged in unison. The bullets fell to the ground, flattened like 30-*sou* pieces.

"Strangle him!" shouted Ozer.

They tried.

The cords broke.

"Drown him!"

A necklace of paving-stones was attached to his neck. He was hauled over the parapet and thrown into the Seine.

There was a shabby mill there, known as the Floating Grinder. Isaac and his paving-stones fell on to the deck-house and rebounded into the river.

182

The band leaned over the parapet to watch.

Isaac's body had disappeared under the water and did not reappear. There was an instant of hope, and Holofernes, always ready with a joke, was preparing a triumphant pun, when a white vapor appeared, floating on the current beside the Pont Saint-Michel. The vapor sheathed a vague form lit by the Sun's rays. It was like the phantom of a girl...

"Ruthael!" exclaimed the false Comte de Savray. He followed the name with an oath that we shall not transcribe, for decency's sake. Ozer was the most foul-mouthed of the Wandering Jews.

At the same time, beneath the white form, the body of a swimmer was discernible, calmly striking out towards the right bank of the river. A long staff floated before him.

"Hellfire!" cried the enraged Ozer.

There was noise and smoke.

The swimmer reached the bank.

Amid the clatter of musketry, the summoning of bells, the clamors of war and the dull booming of cannon, a voice sang:

> *"Death cannot have me,*
> *"I am well aware of that!"*

LXVII. *A Digression in Favor of Playing* Boule 61

Four talents are necessary for playing the game of *boule* with distinction. It is necessary to know how to fetch, to let go, to roll and to aim. Very few people combine all four skills. One alone is sufficient to obtain the esteem of the audience. This art imprints a stamp of innocence on the human physiognomy.

It is said that during those memorable days of July the *boule*-players of the Champs-Elysées did not abandon their beloved game for an instant. There are no longer *boule*-players in the Champs-Elysées. In the place where the "jack" excited such captivating emotions, now stands the ugliest palace in the entire universe. Everything goes–but everything comes around.

The *boule*-players have been dispersed like that Jewish nation of which Ahasuerus, our hero, is the symbolic archetype. Some are "working" at Ranelagh, others in the fields of Beaujon.

In the Avenue de Bel-Air, next to Saint-Mandé, there is a touching spectacle to be seen: a lady–just one– superior to her sex, is admitted to a game of *boule*. She confers upon this hygienic pastime the grace, seriousness, intelligence, delicacy, charm, modesty and tenderness that are the prerogative of her ambition.

I address myself here to the conscience of the people: is that not a better thing than to transform the conjugal roof into a theatre of melodrama?

Music, according to the ancients, could build cities and civilize savage populations. In our modern times, many fine minds think that this role is reserved to the game of *boule*.

A man–or a woman–occupied throughout his or her life in aiming, rolling, letting go and fetching, is sheltered from the tempests of the heart that enervate the wretched children of our sick century.

And since all the writers affirm that not a single *boule*-player left his game in July 1830, nor in February 1848, it is evident that to put an end to the scourge of revolutions, the heroic means would be to make the game of *boule* free of charge and compulsory.

This is what had to be proven.[62]

LXVIII. Through the Iron and Fire of Battalions

Isaac Laquedem climbed up the steps of the Quai des Orfèvres after having passed under the bridge. He was as fresh as a rose and walked at his customary pace, leaning on his long staff.

Having arrived at the corner of the Pont-Neuf, he chanced to be caught in the crossfire of three or four detachments that were exchanging small-talk in the form of rifle-fire. There were dragoons and light infantry on one side; on the other. the regulars at Mother Moreau's [63] and schoolchildren. They were throwing themselves into it, so Isaac Laquedem was severely inconvenienced.

Have you seen hailstones rebounding from the rooftops in March? The bullets did likewise as they touched the Man's rags; he shook them from time to time to disperse the produce of the sudden shower.

The office-boy of the *Journal des Débats*, who had come as far as the end of the Rue des Prêtres to collect a few facts, had an impulse to address the following question to him:

> "*Are you not that man*
> "*Of who so much is said,*
> "*Whom literature names*
> "*Isaac, Wandering Jew...?*"

But he had insufficient time. One of those bullets that could only tickle Isaac struck his peaked cap and blew his brains out. He was a family man. His name is on the column at the Bastille.

As Isaac Laquedem went up towards the Palais-Royal, a house in the Rue de l'Arbre-Sec had the misfortune to collapse on top of him. He was visible for a moment in the midst of the debris. He dusted himself off and went on.

In the very heart of the *Journal des Débats*, in the grave, mildewed, moist, doctrinaire, heretical, upright, accommodating, inflexible and fondant sanctuary where universal sophism is baked, a man, an eye shade, a Doctor, with every last Jansenist hair combed into place, was writing, as impassioned as a *boule*-player, his once-in-a-century article:

"France knows very well that we never change our opinion..."

LXIX. Doctor Lunat's Discovery

It was about 5 p.m. when Isaac Laquedem arrived in the Rue Pierre-Lescot, which was the terminus of his excursion. He had been delayed on his way by saving women, protecting children and helping the wounded. We shall make specific mention only of Doctor Lunat, whom he picked up, pierced by a bayonet-thrust, in the Rue Saint-Honoré, in front of the Laffitte-Caillard Post Office.

This honorable practitioner thanked him very much and said to him:

"I'm on my way, my dear chap, to obtain the proof of a curious particularity. Abbé Romorantin will have the pleasure of jotting it down. It appears–it is Schiavone who mentions it in Note 8, at the end of his second volume–that the Wandering Jew definitely has 24 hours of rest every 100 years. It's not much, but at the end of the day, a little is better than nothing. Schiavone was mad, you know. Bertola too, just like Schedt, and Matthew Paris as well. I've been mad myself; Abbé Romorantin will be too. For every 13 academicians who still pass for sages, there are 14 whose brains..."

Isaac deposited him in the left luggage office.

Then he went to knock on the door of the House of Jews.

LXX. Madame Potiphar

He was let in by Madame Potiphar, the manageress of the establishment, who was extremely worried because none of the various Wandering Jews had returned as yet. Chodruc-Duclos had spent much of the preceding night writing nasty pleasantries to Prince Polignac.

Ahasuerus said a few words to Madame Potiphar, who was somewhat disconcerted by the sight of him.

"We no longer have an empty room, milord," she murmured.

The Man replied: "I want Ozer's lodgings–the one who held out the sponge soaked in vinegar."

Madame Potiphar tried to refuse, but the man murmured in an imperious tone:

"Be quick...

> "*I am sorely annoyed.*
> "*When I am balked!*"

Madame Potiphar obeyed. She took a key from a hook on the wall and went up three floors. She opened a door.

"Go in, milord," she said. "He's been staying here for two days."

The Man went in.

"Now," he commanded, "take the key back and put it on the hook on the wall again..."

"But what if he comes back?"

"He will come back."

"What if he asks for his key?"

"You will give it to him."

"And what shall I say to him?"
"You shall saying nothing to him."

LXXI. The Casket

Madame Potiphar went out. I ought to point out that she was Egyptian, just as Holofernes was Babylonian; Doctor Lunat proves in his great work that there is a considerable mixture in those who are known today as Jews, whether they be wandering or sedentary.

The Man was alone. He sat down in an old armchair and released a voluptuous sigh of relief.

"Well," he murmured, "I'll use up a good part of my 24 hours of rest today. It can't be helped; it's worth the sacrifice."

He crossed his legs and twiddled his thumbs, saying: "It's 17 years since I last played this game. It's pleasant."

The room was wretchedly bare, like all those at the Three Kings. There was no decoration save for a soiled and tattered pictorial print of the Wandering Jew. Isaac looked at it approvingly. *There's a good head on that tankard of beer!* he thought. *I could drink a glass of it with no trouble at all... but these song-merchants make me look too old, my beard too long and my nose too hooked!*

Then he interrupted himself.

"Ah! There's the famous casket!"

His eye had fallen upon a little flat box, half-hidden under the bolster on the bed.

He got up, took it up and opened it, even though it was sealed by a secret catch that would have defied the skill of the best thieves and locksmiths in the capital.

In the little casket, whose interior was exactly similar to the portable pharmacies employed by homeopathic physicians, there were 12 rows of microscopic phials, some of them empty, others containing a colorless liquid.

The phials thus filled numbered 187, the empty ones less than 30.

Which offers firm proof, Isaac thought, smiling, *that my punishment is more than three-quarters complete. The full ones are the past, the empty ones the future. The world has lasted longer than it has to endure.*[64]

He took out all of the phials that were full, one after the other, and examined them attentively in the daylight.

One might have thought that he saw strong likenesses within them.

A few of them drew astonished exclamations from him, as if he had recognized some old acquaintance.

"Well, well!" he said. "There's the secretary to Caligula's horse! [65] Poor chap! Julian the Apostate's barber! [66] One of Fredegonde's cooks! [67] I knew them all: how old that makes me feel! A baron from the time of Philippe-Auguste...[68] The Medicis' chemist...[69] Good old Ravaillac...[70] Cartouche–a good companion! [71] Marat...[72] But where the devil is Sir Arthur, then?"

As the phials were arranged in chronological order, he only fell upon Sir Arthur's at the very end. Immediately after it, came that of Colonel Comte de Savray, after which the series of empty phials began.

Isaac closed the box again and put it back under the bolster.

After that, he lay down on the bed, whose sheets he threw back. He closed his eyes, murmuring:

"Today, I refuse myself nothing: I'll take a little nap."

LXXII. The Wounded Man

The sounds of civil war were fading.

Silence fell gradually upon the city, exhausted by murder, while night cast a veil over the vast scene of carnage.

Isaac Laquedem was asleep. His breathing was as soft and regular as a child's. Penitence is next to innocence.

At his bed head, in the thickening shadow, one might have seen the pale form of a young woman leaning over him, smiling as she maintained her vigil. Innocence protects penitence.

At about 8 p.m., the distant fracas of the battle gave way to other noises. The guests of the House of Jews were returning to the fold, and the party was getting going at Madame Potiphar's.

Isaac half-opened his eyes, listened, turned over and went back to sleep, murmuring:

"I still have three hours."

"For my own part, I shall pray," said the white shadow.

When the Palais-Royal clock chimed 11, heavy footsteps climbed the staircase. The shadow awoke the Man with a kiss and disappeared. At the moment when the key turned in the lock, Isaac was already standing up, hidden behind the curtains.

Two men came in, carrying a wounded man who was deposited on the bed. The false Comte de Savray came in with Herodias, his housekeeper. Then, Doctor

Lunat was led in, his eyes blindfolded and his whole body trembling.

A handkerchief was placed over the face of the wounded man; the Doctor's blindfold was removed and the false Comte said:

"Doctor, you shouldn't judge people by appearances–your visit will earn you ten *louis*. Examine that fellow for me, and tell me whether he'll live."

Aside from certain regions of the brain where he had stars, like you and me, Doctor Lunat was a learned physician. He examined the unconscious man according to the methods of his art.

"He'll live," he pronounced. "I'll answer for him."

Ozer, the false Comte, gave him five double napoleons.[73]

Doctor Lunat took them. He pointed to the picture of the Wandering Jew stuck to the wall.

"That's a copy of the 1790 edition. I'll give you 200 francs for it. Abbé Romorantin has been looking for that version for 20 years..."

The Comte detached the dirty print, gave it to him and showed him out.

There's a funny old fool! the Doctor thought, carrying away his 1790 print.

Ozer ordered a bowl of punch and sat down at the table with Herodias.

"We have three-quarters of an hour to wait," he said. "I can't do the operation until midnight sounds. Let's chat."

LXXIII. The Great Secret

"When our glasses are full, my queen," the false Comte continued, "I'll tell you the full story."

"Can't I stay here during the operation?" Herodias asked. "I'd like to watch."

"No, impossible. I have to be alone. That's the law. But I can enable you to be present in spirit..."

"I want to watch!" Herodias interrupted, obstinately.

"Only the King says, I want," Ozer the soldier pronounced, solemnly. Then, with a gross laugh, he added: "And yet, they don't obey him every day." He drank a glass of punch and continued: "We're alone. The wounded man is unconscious. That fool of a Doctor didn't even think of trying to bring him round. We can chat; it'll kill the time–and whenever I have to exchange bodies, I always feel a little natural emotion..."

"It's dangerous, then?" Herodias asked.

"My God, no–quite the contrary... but it's delicate. This is how it is: I have to have an unconscious man, because he must be completely in my power, but a man in good health, because I wouldn't want to enfeeble myself with a body that's disabled or in danger of death. When I took over Sir Arthur, I simply gave him a glass of wine to drink that had a strong dose of laudanum in it. When I introduced myself into the skin of Colonel Comte de Savray..."

"You'll miss that body!" Herodias put in. "Five feet seven inches, and a cushy billet!"

"It's possible, but let me tell you this little story. It was the night of the fire, out there in Tours. While that rogue Ahasuerus was saving the child, I was close behind the father. The light of the fire was dazzling, and his head was all over the place anyhow. He stumbled over a fireman's hose; I thumped him with my fist, and while he was trying to get up, his senses reeling like a drunkard's, I slowly inhaled his soul, and moved into him as if I were coming home."

"It's astonishing, all the same," said Queen Herodias. "I'd like to see it!"

"And I went back to the calèche," Ozer added, "to stretch myself out beside Comtesse Louise, who was now my legitimate wife."

"Did she fall into the trap?"

"Bah!" said Ozer. "The harpy never let me kiss her fingertips."

LXXIV. Midnight

The first stroke of midnight sounded from the neighboring bell-towers. The soldier Ozer hurriedly got up and shoved Herodias towards the door. The dregs of the punch-bowl were drained.

Left alone, Ozer went to the wounded man and examined him.

"A handsome chap!" he said. "Son of the richest banker in the liberal party. I'll make an immense fortune and get a foothold in the new Court."

He took the little casket, selected from it the phial next to the one containing the soul of Colonel Comte de Savray, and pounced on the wounded man with a snarl of joy.

His lips adhered to the mouth of the young man; he breathed deeply and put the mouth of the little phial to his lips, in order to breathe out the stolen soul.

The filled phial was restoppered. It now contained the soul of the wounded man.

"Farewell, my carcase!" Ozer said, at the same time.

His body–the former body of the Comte de Savray–fell like a dead weight. A strange, monstrous form seemed to disengage itself from the cadaver. This form bounded towards the wounded man, who was himself no more than a corpse awaiting another soul to revivify it.

At that very moment, however, a hand of iron seized the monster by the hair and threw it back to the other side of the room.

The monster stared.

"Ahasuerus!" it said. "Oh, cunning Ahasuerus!"

197

It let loose a terrible howl and threw itself forwards, head bowed.

Its head met the Man's breast. It sounded as if it had run into a stone wall.

"For pity's sake!" said the monster. "The hour has sounded! If I don't get into that body right away, it will die–and me with it!"

The Man folded his arms across his chest and remained silent.

"For pity's sake! For pity's sake!"

Then blasphemies, and a gnashing of teeth.

The monster writhed like a wounded snake.

A few moments later, the silence of death reigned in the room, where there were three corpses: that of Colonel Comte de Savray, that of the liberal banker's son–and that of Ozer, who had once been King Herod's soldier. The sounds of the drunken orgy continued on the floor below.

LXXV. Explanations

Doctor Lunat, Member of the Institute, had certainly been wrong, professionally speaking, not to have restored the use of his senses to the son of the richest liberal banker–but one cannot think of everything, and the Doctor's attention had naturally been monopolized by the print of the Wandering Jew, the 1790 edition. It is necessary to excuse the illustrious alienist. Without his immense labors, conducted with the aid of the good Abbé Romorantin, our story would be full of implausibilities and lacunae.

It is well-established–is it not?–that the world has grown old, and that it is letting out its secrets like an old man in his second childhood. We have recently learned the real name of Mathieu Laensberg,[74] the benevolent father of almanacs, occupied throughout the centuries in predicting day by day the weather that God need not make. An illustrious medium has avowed, while weeping, that he was Joseph Balsamo,[75] who bitterly regretted the mischief of his younger days. We have seen the Cumaean Sibyl [76] found guilty at the court of summary jurisdiction, and Apollonius of Tyana [77] in his conjuror's booth on the boulevard, where one sees him change bodies and names every seven years.

This is a matter of fact; we have it from Doctor Lunat, whose competence can scarcely be challenged: in principle, Herod's soldier, Ozer, had three minutes to contrive the removals of his soul. Once this time was past, if the soul fell between two stools, it died.

Is it possible, though, for a soul to die?

Schiavone, quoted by the Scotsman Lockhard, affirms it–but they are not reliable. El Edrisi prefers to doubt that Ozer's soul is truly a soul. I recommend Schedt on the matter. He knows nothing about it, but he is a Tyrolean, and he has a good heart.

The soul does not die, except for the terrible death of which the Scriptures speak, which is eternal punishment–but wicked men die, even those to whom celestial patience has granted these long respites that astonish the centuries.

LXXVI. The Death of Madame Herodias

Isaac Laquedem nudged the monster with his foot to as-
certain whether it was really deceased, after which he
carefully put the soul of the wounded young businessman back into his body. This seemed to comfort him–the
young businessman, that is.

Isaac then took a handkerchief and knotted its four
corners together, in order to place the cadaver of Colonel
Comte de Savray within it. It is unnecessary to remark
that this could not have been done without some mildly
supernatural contrivance. Nevertheless, it was not as miraculous as you might think. The body lent itself to this
operation by shrinking, shrinking, shrinking... we shall
explain that fact scientifically in a subsequent chapter,
entitled *The Theory of Limbo.*[78]

Isaac Laquedem put the little box containing the
phials into his pocket. This was significant to what followed.

He told the young businessman, the son of one of
the richest liberal bankers, to get up. The young businessman got up, without neglecting to pass his hands
over his eyes and murmur:

"Where am I?"

Isaac Laquedem took up his staff and opened the
door. Herodias was on the other side of it, her eye glued
to the keyhole in order to satisfy her guilty curiosity.
Isaac knocked her out with a single blow of the thick
end.

He went into the room where the various Wandering Jews were making merry, and massacred as many as
he could with blows of his staff. Chodruc-Duclos alone

escaped the carnage, because he had gone to sing a sere-
nade beneath the windows of the Prince de Polignac.

All these murders passed unnoticed, by courtesy of
the civil war. Besides, every one of these brave Israelites
had already been broken on the wheel, hung, executed
by firing-squad and guillotined several times over, at
various times. All of them are in the best of health as we
inscribe these lines.

The liberal banker's son was returned to his family.
His name became famous in association with one of the
greatest bankruptcies of the century, fecund with peril-
ous plunges.

LXXVII. A Breath of Hope

As midnight sounded at the Church of Notre-Dame-des-Champs–which is to say, at the precise moment when Isaac Laquedem, the living penitence of 18 centuries, exterminated the monster that had been the soldier Ozer, the shameful and degraded image of unrepentant crime–Comtesse Louise felt that a weight had been lifted from her heart.

She was there, at the bedside of the sleeping Vicomte Paul. Vicomte Paul was smiling. His pale hand was between the hands of the beautiful, white and gentle young woman who resembled little Lotte.

In the next room, Fanchon the nurse and the good Abbé Romorantin were talking about surprising things. Abbé Romorantin was telling Fanchon that Ahasuerus' daughter was a duplicate... yes, you read it correctly: duplicate. It's no more incredible that the rest of the story.

It has been observed that the white hand that was touching the hand of Vicomte Paul was sowing his slumber with pleasant dreams.

Comtesse Louise looked at them in turn, her memory climbing the slopes of the past again. She astonished herself by no longer finding them flooded with tears.

A few minutes after midnight, the beautiful young woman's lips opened slightly to let fall these words, suspended like pearls from her smile:

"*My Father is coming.*"

At the same time, sonorous footsteps began to sound on the pavement in the street. Comtesse Louise went to the window and saw a man of tall stature who was walking in the shadows, leaning on a long staff. The wind that stirred the man's hair seemed to carry a perfume of hope...

When Louise closed the casement again, Vicomte Paul had woken up.

"Mother," he said, "I dreamed that my father was embracing me–my father from the other time; my true father!"

LXVIII. The Route de Flandres

We are on the Route de Flandres. The Man is striding forth; the Moon illuminates his upright and robust figure. The breath emerges strongly from his lungs.

Already, behind him, the gigantic perspectives of Paris are lost in the night–a Paris changed into an armed camp, sleeping the feverish slumber of civil war.

On the summit of the hill at Livry, the Man turned round. His eyes saw further and more clearly than those of other men because, despite the distance, he could make out an old man on watch, alone and pensive, in a room in the Tuileries palace. That palace had seen a great many similar vigils.

The old man was a King.

"March! March!" murmured the Man. "Do as I do, unquiet century, valiant people, sick humanity! March! March! March!"

He went on his silent and rapid way. The trees fled behind him; the distant bell-towers grew, then passed by.

A white form glided beside him, never quitting him, any more than his shadow did.

When the light of dawn appeared, a vast forest draped around him the inclined planes of a mountain range. He had crossed the French frontier; it was German territory that now surrounded him.

LXXIX. The Theory of Limbo

By 6 a.m., Isaac Laquedem was in the Hartz Mountains, descending the steep slopes of the Andreasberg. The forest echoes were awakened by the howling of the stag hounds of the former privy councilor, Baron von Pfifferlackentrontonstein, who had still not cornered the hind that had put him off the track during our first visit to this wild landscape. He was still chasing her.

"Ruthael," said Isaac, "are we on the right road to Three Wells?"

"We're there, Father," replied the white vision.

Indeed, a short while afterwards, the basket descended into the bowels of the Earth with Isaac Laquedem in it.

We have only half a page here to elucidate a question that would take up 12 quarto volumes of the great work of Doctor Lunat, relating to the hypothetical stations of souls. That learned man was not a materialist; he admitted five stations, two of them eternal—Heaven and Hell—and three transitory: Earth, Purgatory and Limbo.

Limbo is upon and below the Earth; the Earth contains everything, except Heaven and Hell.

Those whose bodies had been stolen by the soldier Ozer were vegetating in Limbo, according to the Doctor's Theory. By means of what bodies, though, since Herod's soldier had appropriated theirs for his own use and kept their souls in little bottles? There are enormous problems here; properly speaking, there are neither bodies nor souls in Limbo.

Visit certain factories in London—for a full third of that free city is in Limbo—and search for bodies and souls there! Bodies, one can find: degenerate bodies horrible misshapen by industrial oppression. But souls... I swear that there are none there!

I have seen with my own eyes, in London, a victim of Ozer, who has been creeping through the same subterranean passage for 17 years, pushing the same wagon along the same rails. He is no longer anything but a machine, and that machine has forgotten its own name. It knows but one god: the overseer's dog that bays behind it whenever the wagon comes to a halt.

Nine hundred meters below the sunlit ground, the remains or reflections of the real Sir Arthur and the real Colonel Comte Roland de Savray, miserable things that no longer had souls in their beaten-down bodies, were vegetating in the depths of the Andreasberg mines–in Limbo.

This Sir Arthur, we ought to emphasize, was not the English villain that we met at Tours in Touraine, but the other one–the one who left his box at the theatre one night and who was swindled out of his soul in the corridors–in a word, the penultimate victim of the soldier Ozer, since Comte Roland was the last.

LXXX. Firedamp [79]

He and the Comte were both hewing the rock-face, sadly, silently, doubled over with fatigue and discouragement, next to a pool of water darker than Erebus.[80] Their lanterns were smoking at their feet. Momentarily, they paused and looked at one another. There were burning tears in their eyes.

"I can't go on!" said the Comte, throwing away his pickaxe.

Sir Arthur did likewise, and added: "I'd rather die!"

They sat down, side by side, on the damp ground, their hands folded and their expressions vague.

"Do you still remember," Sir Arthur asked, "what you were before?"

"I don't know," Vicomte Paul's father replied. "I try to remember... it seems to me... but no... I've forgotten everything!"

They put their numbed heads between their trembling hands.

"Let's go, lazybones!" cried the loud voice of the overseer.

But they made no move to get up.

There were threats and cracks of the whip. They remained motionless.

At that moment, distant voices—ominous voices—were heard, their cries inarticulate at first but becoming more distinct, saying:

"Put the lights out! Firedamp!"

A cascade of overseers began running. The miners left their work, the row of extinguished lights coming closer and closer along the subterranean corridor.

A grey vapor, like a gauze, was seeping out of the depths of the mine.

And beyond that vapor a man of tall stature could be seen, who was supporting himself with his staff as he walked. At his side, a child was gliding through the darkness.

"Extinguish the lamps! Fire! Firedamp!"

In those hidden cities, there is no order as rapidly carried out as that. A lighted lantern, when that grey vapor extends like a floculant veil and reaches the height of a man, is death itself.

All the lights went out, one after the other.

With two exceptions, which shone in the lanterns of Vicomte Paul's father and Sir Arthur.

The overseers were running away; the tall man was approaching–but between the two, the grey vapor arrived.

The vapor touched one of the lanterns. A dry explosion tore through the air, which swelled up as it incited echoes, prolonging its awful noise into the distant galleries. There was a loud cry, followed by a deep silence.

All those who had formerly been standing were lying on the ground, immobile–and dead.

Except for the tall figure of the stranger, who remained upright on his feet, and the little girl he held by the hand.

LXXXI. *The Souls*

The stranger leaned over Comte Roland de Savray, then over Sir Arthur; both of them seemed deprived of life. He opened Ozer's box, full of souls, and selected two phials, which he put to their lips.

"I warnt to go to Paris roight away," Sir Arthur declared, immediately, as he got up. "I warnt to say the tredgedy."

And Vicomte Paul's father, feeling himself like one emerging from a dream:

"Louise! My darling wife! Paul! My beloved son! Where are they? Where are they?"

The maniac English soul.

The good soul of France, which, if only it can be reawakened, makes a good heart beat!

LXXXII. Goodbyes

On a splendid August day, the setting Sun inflamed the gracious curve of the Seine at the foot of the Meudon hill.

In the living-room of a charming cottage, whose windows overlooked the river, Colonel Comte Roland de Savray, as brilliant as before, was chatting with Comtesse Louise in a window-bay. Roland applied his lips to his wife's hands, beautified by happiness.

Vicomte Paul, who no longer felt his wound, was next to Lotte, as gentle as a saint. They were talking about their forthcoming union.

The good Abbé Romorantin was trying to obtain some very delicate information from a man of tall stature who was standing in the middle of the room, staff in hand.

Through the open door, the curious faces of the nurse Fanchon and the hussar Joli-Coeur could be seen.

The church bell struck six times.

Isaac Laquedem said:

"My friends, I must say my good-byes. My 24 hours of leave is used up."

Everyone immediately surrounded him, while Fanchon sang:

> *"Gentlemen, time presses me*
> *"Farewell to the company.*
> *"By grace of your civility*
> *"I owe you many thanks..."*

"What, already!" cried Comtesse Louise, clasping Isaac's hands.

"It's necessary," he replied. "I've been summoned."

"By whom?" asked the Comte.

"The Angel," Isaac replied, leaning over Lotte to kiss the forehead of the young bride-to-be.

Lotte smiled. The others had tears in their eyes.

"I want to pray to the Angel," cried Vicomte Paul, "that he might let you remain with us! What is his name?"

"His name is Expiation."

Isaac was already on the threshold of the room. His hand touched his lips and sent a kiss to all those he loved.

He was soon visible on the high road that ran alongside the river. The setting Sun played upon the sparse strands of his hair.

"Lotte!" exclaimed Paul, suddenly–for he had just perceived a little white shadow walking by the traveler's side behind the Angel, minister of the infinite mercy of the Good Lord. "Lotte! Don't abandon me!"

"I'm here," a soft voice responded, "at your side."

"You can clearly see that she is a duplicate!" the good Abbé Romorantin murmured in Fanchon's ear. "Behold a fact acquired by science!"

The traveler turned the corner of the towpath and disappeared behind the poplars. The evening breeze carried back the words of his sad, soft song:

> "*The last judgment*
> "*Will end my torment...*"

Afterword

As was pointed out in the introduction, *The Wandering Jew's Daughter* is to some extent a companion-piece to *Knightshade*, the latter being set on the eve of the July Revolution of 1830 while the heart of the former is a description of the state of Paris during the first days of the event. In order to appreciate the text fully, it is necessary to know something about the particular personal significance of that event to Paul Féval.

By the time Paul Féval wrote *The Wandering Jew's Daughter*, he knew that the July Revolution of 1830 was the middle item in a set of three, and thus regarded it as one of a frustratingly repetitive series, but it had not seemed so at the time, when he lived through it at a significant point in his life. Féval, like his namesake in the story, was an adolescent in 1830, prematurely enrolled at the University of Rennes following the death of his father and the further reduction of his mother's already-straitened circumstances. (Like Comtesse Louise in the story, Féval's mother had aristocratic connections that were no longer of any material use to her, although young Paul got to spend his vacations at the country estate of a titled cousin.)

The University became so turbulent during the July Revolution, as its personnel separated into factions, that teaching was suspended and the students were sent home. Young Paul Féval was a Bourbon-supporting *légitimiste*, and thus in the minority–a position that must have seemed absurd to many of his fellow students, given that he was the son of a lawyer whose mother and sisters were living in poverty. The scorn implicit in that opinion, one presumes, must have made Féval cling even harder to his own views, and there is probably a echo of it in the scene in which Paul is goaded into a duel when the scorn of his fellow pupils extends to an insult to his mother. Unlike Vicomte Paul, though, Paul Féval was not yet 14 in July 1830, and not in any position to defend his mother's honor.

Reading the accounts of Vicomte Paul's unfortunate fall in the wake of the catastrophic loss of his home and his father, and the subsequent derision he incurs from his fellow students, one can hardly help feeling that Féval is allegorizing his own situation in *The Wandering Jew's Daughter* as well as that of France. If so, it is interesting that Paul de Savray is virtually forgotten during the novel's climax, lying impotently wounded in his bed while Ahasuerus bears witness to the Revolution and moves towards a belated final reckoning with Ozer. Paul's story is given a conclusion of sorts, but it is equally interesting that the mysteries introduced in the first few chapters are never wholly resolved.

It seems obvious, in the build-up to the fire, that it is Paul himself who precipitates the disaster, by causing the violation of an injunction that the Wandering Jew's name must never be spoken in the house, but this is never fully explained. Readers are similarly left to draw their own conclusions about the precise reason for the unageing Lotte's presence in the house, and her status within it. One thing that is certain, however, is that from the personal viewpoint of Vicomte Paul, if not the reader, the key symbolic character in the story is not Ahasuerus at all, but Lotte. That is presumably why, having tested out two other titles, Féval finally settled on the one that I have retained in this translation.

In drawing parallels between Paul Féval's memories of his own childhood and that of Vicomte Paul, perhaps it ought not to be forgotten that, in 1864, there was a third Paul to be taken into account: Paul Féval's eldest son, who was eventually to embark upon a literary career of his own as Paul Féval *fils*. The younger Paul Féval had been born on January 25, 1860, so he would have been four years old when *The Wandering Jew's Daughter* was written and published–not too young to be read to, but far too young to understand a narrative as sophisticated as this. The younger Paul had been preceded into the world by two sisters; the elder, born in December 1854, would have been nine–two years younger than Vicomte Paul–when the novella was published.

Galvan does not record the birth-date of the second daughter, nor the death-dates of any of the eight children to whom Françoise Féval eventually gave birth, but he does record that the elder Paul Féval also had two older sisters (plus two older brothers) and that a third, Virginie, had died in infancy. Paul would have had no memory of Virginie, but that does not mean that she could not have had a presence of sorts in his life. If she had, the notion of a ghostly child who does not age might take on a new significance–and it is conceivable the personal significance of such an image might have been renewed by 1864, by anxiety if not by actuality. The elder Paul Féval must, however, have had occasion to wish–however guiltily–that he had been an only son, with none but ghostly siblings for company.

Although *The Wandering Jew's Daughter* is not short of innovations, some of which anticipate later developments in popular fiction–in his capacity as an invulnerable (but flawed) superhero who stops bullets and blades with his body and gives succor to the wounded, the Wandering Jew adds another item to an already-extensive catalogue of Féval's anticipations of modern comic book mythology–it is Lotte who is the novella's most interesting invention. It is her role as a consoler, of her father and of Paul, that is eventually crucial to the novella's emotional tone, and it is the nature of her character, more exotic even than Ozer's, that provides the story with its most engaging enigma.

Oddly enough, given the innovative nature of Féval's novella, Lotte is not without literary precedent. It is highly unlikely that Féval had ever encountered the other notable tale that equips an Accursed Wanderer with a companion daughter, because it appeared in the USA, but the similarities between Lotte and her predecessor are intriguing nevertheless. The earlier example is found in "*Peter Rugg, the Missing Man*" by William Austin (1788-1841), originally published in 1824 but further expanded in 1827. (Its near-contemporary setting thus overlaps the time-scheme of Féval's novella.)

In Austin's novella, an inquisitive New Yorker investigates the strange case of Peter Rugg, an Accursed Wanderer who has been trying in vain to reach his home in Boston for 50 years, driving his uncovered carriage feverishly along the local roads while being pursued by a perversely localized storm. Rugg is accompanied on his bare chassis by his hapless daughter, Jenny. The first part of the story explains how the narrator first encountered these strange individuals, and then made inquiries as to their story, learning that Rugg was on his way home from Concord one night in 1770 when he was overtaken by a violent storm, but insisted on continuing his return journey, swearing a "terrible" oath that he would reach home that night, or never. The second part of the story describes a meeting in Richmond, Virginia, when Rugg's seemingly-diabolical horse outgallops two noted racehorses, and a ride through New York–a city in which Rugg can hardly believe, having no knowledge of the "United States"–before concluding with an auction of Rugg's long-derelict property in Boston, during which the Wanderer finally reaches his destination (after an absence of 55 years), only to learn that his home no longer exists.

Like Washington Irving's accounts of "*Rip van Winkle*" and "*The Legend of Sleepy Hollow*" (1819-20), the tale of Peter Rugg is an Americanization of a European legend, modeled on the story of the Flying Dutchman. The period of Rugg's exile is, however, a crucial epoch in American history, and his alienation from the course of events is all the greater for his ignorance of the Revolution that has taken place in the interim. While his mistaken roads gradually take him further and further afield, into a new nation that is growing and flourishing, he remains becalmed in his personal pre-Revolutionary backwater; Rugg is a "missing man" because of what he misses rather than because he is missed.

The more puzzling figure in Rugg's story, if it is to be considered as an allegory, is that of Jenny, who never uttered any kind of oath but has had to endure her father's storm-tossed fate regardless, wretchedly stuck at ten years of age for more than half a century. This seems blatantly unjust–all the more so as Jenny's plight remains conspicuously unconsidered in the second part of the story. It seems that Austin has forgotten all about her, although the reader is free to reflect that she must have had far more scope for reintegrating herself into the stream of history than her father. Precisely because she is a child, she still has time enough–and certainly has motive enough–to grow up to be a good American.

To some extent, the same considerations that apply to Jenny Rugg apply to Ruthael/Lotte. She never did anything to offend Christ, so it seems frankly unjust that she should be forced to share her father's fate–especially as any siblings she may have had (presumably we ought to accept Doctor Lunat's judgment that her mother was already dead when her father was condemned) were obviously not permitted to add to the family unit. Ruthael is, one must suppose, condemned by love; like Quinet's Rachel, she has apparently elected to share the Wanderer's fate in order to relieve a little of his burden. It is a fate from which she cannot be liberated, even though she is free to fall in love with a mere mortal; when she marries Paul, she must also remain with her father, dividing herself in two. Unlike Jenny Rugg, only a part of Ruthael/Lotte can rejoin the stream of time, to grow up and grow old; the other part must remain existentially marooned.

Given that all this must logically be the case, however, why was an ageless fraction of Ruthael/Lotte ever detached from her father in Lamballe? Can what Monsieur Galapian told Madame Lancelot about her being handed over as a good-luck charm really be true, given what we are subsequently told and shown regarding the relationship between father and daughter? If not, what was she doing in the Savray household at the story's beginning? Why did she fade away as soon as the headstrong Paul broke the taboo against speaking her father's name? What actually happened on that fateful night in Lamballe, to which Madame Lancelot was only a distant witness? Why does Féval continually refer to the Colonel Comte's addiction to gambling, as if to imply that it had something to do with his sudden good fortune? Was the dying Jew's arrival at the Savrays' house on the night when Louise was due to give birth more than mere coincidence–and, if so, what is the connection between Paul's birth and the Jew's regeneration?

There can be no definitive answer to these questions, because the text only treats them elliptically–almost everything we know about such matters comes from potentially-unreliable second-hard reporting–but we are, as ever, free to speculate. One suspicion we might entertain is that Féval changed his mind about certain aspects of his plot–or introduce new ones he had not previously thought about–between the end of Chapter XXX and the beginning of Chapter XXXI. Given that he was such a fast writer, it is not implausible that that interval might have been the break between his first day's work and his second, when a plot that was being made up as it went along might easily change direction.

Although he seems in the latter part of the novel to be invulnerable to all injury, and miraculously strong (he walks all the way from Paris to the Hartz mountains in the space of a single day!), Féval's Ahasuerus obviously has far worse days, when Ruthael has to help him out–as she does when she descends into the mine in search of the Comte and Sir Arthur. Even if the rumor is true that he is bound to die once in every 100 years, he surely could not have come to a final end had the Savrays not taken him, but he really does seem to have been suffering and the Savrays clearly alleviated that suffering, thus facilitating his self-renewal. After Chapter XXX, however, we learn that it was not, however, Ahasuerus/Isaac Laquedem who acquired a new body that night, but Ozer, who took possession of the Colonel's father (a character unmentioned by Madame Lancelot).

One might suspect that, when he wrote his account of the usurpation of the body of the Colonel's father–which is credited to the narrative voice, even though the situation is set up to report it as conversation between Fanchon and Joli-Coeur–Féval had only just decided that there were to be two Wandering Jews. Why else was only one person seen entering the house in Lamballe? Long before the end of Chapter XXX, it is obvious that Sir Arthur is to be the plot's villain, but it is not until after that juncture that the precise nature of his villainy becomes clear; before the fire, his chief sin seems to be lechery, but afterwards, the possibility of his making free with the lovely Comtesse is quickly set aside.

It seems likely that Féval had at least considered the possibility that the Savrays had been rewarded for their trouble by a simple transfer of funds amassed by the method sketched out in Doctor Lunat's anecdote about the effects of a hole in the pocket on his ever-renewing five *sous*. It also seems likely that he had considered the possibility of involving some kind of wager (why else take such trouble to establish that Comte Roland was a gambling man?). Given that he also took the trouble to have Madame Lancelot introduced the possibility that Ahasuerus gave the Savrays a good-luck charm–apparently in connection with a warning, of a kind customary in folk tales, that they would lose it if ever they broke an associated injunction. If he ever settled on one of these three possibilities, he never took the trouble to spell it out in any detail, and one suspects that he did not, allowing himself to be carried away instead by the new ideas he imported into the lot on the second day of composition.

We, as readers, are bound to favor the third possibility–that he did indeed leave his beloved Lotte behind as a token of his indebtedness, which did indeed vanish when the injunction was broken, apparently causing 11 years' defiance of the laws of chance to unravel in a hurry, precipitating a compensatory avalanche of ill-fortune. Perhaps, though, we ought also to consider the possibility that, in his original plan, Féval had not intended to make his two Wandering Jews so decisively distinct. Perhaps we only heard from Madame Lancelot of one Jew arriving at the Lamballe house because there was only one in Féval's mind at the time, who contained both Ahasuerus and Ozer–and perhaps the Savrays paid more dearly for their reward than was apparent to Madame Lancelot. Perhaps the traveler with the staff and Sir Arthur only seemed to be two different individuals on the night of the fire, and Roland's father had to pay for the rescue of his son with his own body.

If something of the sort was ever in his mind, Féval obviously changed it in the course of the narrative, contriving a Manichean split between the good and evil aspects of the character, glossing over Ahasuerus' need for periodic renewal and increasing Ozer's similar need to intervals of less than a decade (although the arithmetic, as the notes point out, is a trifle inconsistent).

If Féval did start out with the assumption that Ahasuerus and Ozer were different aspects of the same individual, then it is conceivable that the individual in question was, in fact, a trinity, and that Ruthael too ought to be reckoned part of the collective: a kind of Holy Ghost (in the language of the Authorized Version). This is an admittedly bizarre suggestion, despite the continual representation of Ruthael as an elusive phantom, but it may be worth noting that the story does take great care to introduce the image of the three magi who were present at the birth of Jesus, in circumstances faintly echoed in the birth of Vicomte Paul, and that one of the chapter-headings dealing with the collapse of the Savrays' good fortune refers, enigmatically, to "a confusion of tongues" (in Acts 2:4-8 an intervention of the Holy Ghost clears up exactly such a confusion, so one might logically expect its withdrawal to have an opposite effect). If Féval had some such allegorical scheme in mind, however, he disposed of it once the fire from which Paul is miraculously saved had run its course. From that moment on, Ozer is a completely distinct individual.

Or is he?

This may seem like a stupid question, given that the narrative voice leaves us in no doubt of the fact, and I would not dream of questioning it had I not been the translator of *Jean Diable* (1862; tr. as *John Devil*) in which there is a suspiciously similar confusion between good and evil characters who begin as two aspects of the same individual but end up crudely (and unconvincingly) cloven in two. Throughout his career, Féval was preoccupied with dual personalities–but he never explicitly contrived a fusion as intimate as that of Edgar Allan Poe's two aspects of "*William Wilson*" or Robert Louis Stevenson's *Dr. Jekyll and Mr. Hyde*, although he does seem to have toyed with the idea on more than one occasion.

If it were a character rather than the narrative voice who tells the reader about the Wandering Jew's odyssey through the barricades, and his confrontation with Ozer in the phantasmagoric House of Jews, we would be every bit as skeptical of it as we are of Doctor Lunat's account of the endless amplification of the five *sous*. The account of bouncing bullets and glancing blades would seem preposterous, and the story of the casket full of phials an obvious invention. It would all seem like a dream–and perhaps that is the best way to regard it: as a flight of deeply perverse wish-fulfillment fantasy that took hold of the writer as he wrote, and transformed his original intention without his being able to make sense of it.

Perhaps, in that case, Ahasuerus' symbolic destruction of Ozer is a belated rejection of his own dark half–an action that goes beyond mere repentance of his sin to the actual conquest of evil: a kind of revolution that actually works. Féval, the royalist enemy of revolutions, could never openly admit that, of course. This Ahasuerus is condemned by the faith that Féval could never quite be rid of to return to his eternal *complainte* and go on and on, expecting no change in his condition until the world ends (in 2100 or thereabouts, according to Féval's apparent estimation). Like everyone else, however, we are free to imagine a different future for the luckless Wanderer, in which the world does not end at all, and in which the destruction of Ozer sets him free to make something new of himself. After all, even if he still cannot make a home in such a doomless world, his loving daughter might still be free to grow up entirely, no longer sacrificing anything of her own identity to his frustrating and futile punishment. She deserves that, doesn't she?

Notes

[1] Etienne Bezout (1784-1783) was a noted French mathematician who designed the mathematics course for the Ecole Polytechnique (six vols., 1780).

[2] There is no exact English equivalent of the *images à un sou* that Fanchon collects, but the "broadside ballads" that flourished in the same period were similar, supplementing a gaudy illustration with a text, usually in rhyme. Fanchon's are, as we shall see, pocket-sized when rolled up, accumulated like decks of cards; she would have bought them from *colporteurs* (itinerant peddlers). The illustrated verses such prints contained were formulated to be sung to popular tunes. The town of Epinal in northeastern France, whose print-works was the chief source of these images in the 18th and 19th centuries, has a museum devoted to their history, in which the print of the Wandering Jew may still be seen.

[3] The titan Cronus–identified by the Romans with Saturn–was warned by his mother Gaea that he was destined to be deposed by one of the children he fathered on his sister and wife Rhea, so he swallowed them all. When Zeus, identified by the Romans with Jupiter–was born, Rhea hid him on Crete, where he was raised in secret until he was able to depose his father and institute the rule of the gods. The Corybants, mythical attendants of the Greek mother-goddess Cybele–who was eventually fused with Rhea–were supposed to accompany her with wild songs and dances as she wandered the forested mountains; their actions were allegedly simulated by Cybele's priests in orgiastic rites.

[4] Belshazzar (Féval has Balthasar, but I have substituted the form of the name used in the Authorized Version, as with all other Biblical names) was the King of Babylon at whose notorious feast–described in Daniel 5–the proverbial writing on the

wall appeared, prophesying the destruction of his Kingdom on account of his having been "weighed in the balance and found wanting."

[5] In French, *Terre* (Earth) rhymes with *Misère* (Misery) and *Surprenant* (Amazing) with the unvoiced *Juif Errant* (Wandering Jew). In citing the verses of the Brabantine ballad at the various points in the text at which they crop up, I have made no attempt to reproduce the scansion, or the rhyme-scheme, because any such contrivance would inevitably have distorted the meanings of lines, whose principal charm derives from their simplicity.

[6] "*Vive la charte, à bas le charretier!*" sounds better in French than in English, although the pun does translate.

[7] The Abbé is referring to the last syllable of the third line, which is supposed to rhyme with the *proteste* at the end of the first. Many old French words including the intermediate formulation "*est*" contracted it in modern French to "*êt*" (*fenêtre* is the most familiar example). The version of the third line given by Féval ends in *arrête*–which is, indeed, a false rhyme.

[8] Féval's use of Matthew Paris' name creates a gloss of scholarly authenticity that disguises the fabrication of all the names that follow, with the possible exception of Schedt, which might conceivably be a misrendering of the name of Johann Jacob Schudt (whose scholarly contribution to the history of the legend was the notion that it was a symbolic representation of the plight of the Jewish people in the wake of the diaspora). Féval's reference to a scholar named Schiavone is slightly odd, given that name would have been familiar to some readers as the pseudonym of the 16th-century Italian painter Andrea Meldolla, but this is presumably a coincidence.

[9] As explained in the introduction, this reference is obviously to the version of the story coined by Marana, but I have retained Féval's spelling rather than substituting Marana's Ader because Féval's version of the character is very much his own invention.

[10] *Vade retro* [*Satanas*] is the Latin version of Jesus' response to temptation, given in the Authorized Version as "*Get thee hence, Satan!*" (Matthew 4:10) but popularly rendered as "*Get thee behind me, Satan!*"

[11] This is a play on words, *souci* (marigold) also meaning care or worry, while *rose* has similar metaphorical connotations in French and English.

[12] Napoleon's servant Roustan (1780-1845) was a minor celebrity of the era. The mamelukes were an Egyptian cavalry unit initially made up of slaves–mostly, like Roustan, from the Causasus–although their leaders were rulers of Egypt for some while before it became part of the Ottoman Empire; they suffered a crucial defeat by Napoleon at the battle of the pyramids in 1798 and were exterminated in 1811 when the Turks reclaimed their losses.

[13] I have left *sylphide* in French rather than translating it as sylph because the term is now well known, especially with reference to dancing, by virtue of Schneitzhoffer's Paris-produced ballet *La Sylphide* (1832). Féval presumably has that ballet in mind, although the Brigade Commander's reference to it is flagrantly anachronistic. (Maria Taglioni, who made the lead part her own, did not leave the stage until 1847, so Féval may conceivably have seen her.) There was also a Parisian periodical called *La Sylphide*, to which Féval contributed in the early days of his career.

¹⁴ Féval was exceedingly fond of making jokes about the poor quality of contemporary Suresnes wine; this slight is typical.

¹⁵ François-Joseph Talma (1763-1826) was the foremost tragic actor of the period encompassing both the Revolution to the Restoration. He introduced to the French stage the custom of wearing the costume of the period in which the play is set. His first great triumph, in 1789, was as Charles IX; although his Caesar was also legendary, the reference to the "immemorial Augustus" is ironic–as is almost everything else in the lunatic Doctor's discourse.

¹⁶ The Salpêtrière was a hospital for women incapacitated by age and mental illness.

¹⁷ Alphonse-Louis-Dieudonné Martainville (1776-1830) was a journalist and playwright noted for his far right politics (Larousse describes him as "more royalist than the King"). His greatest literary success was a play called *Le Pied du Mouton* (1807), one of a series of fantastic comedies begun with *La Tête du Diable, ou le Flambeau de l'Amour* (1807).

¹⁸ At the time when Féval wrote *La Fille de Juif Errant* (but not in the era in which the story is set), *Le Nain Jaune* was a Parisian periodical edited by the poet and novelist Aurélien Scholl, whose political and religious ideas were flatly opposed to Féval's. It was named after Madame d'Aulnoy's famous fairy tale (known in English as *The Yellow Dwarf*); even had it existed under the Restoration, it would not have had a provincial offshoot (the Indre is a district through which the Loire flows) so this reference is merely a joke.

¹⁹ The *Ambiliati* (Féval has *Ambiliates*) were a Celtic tribe mentioned in Caesar's *Gallic Wars* as living in Brittany, but the inference that they must have been the rulers of the region was drawn at a later date by Bretons in quest of their history;

there is no further reference to them in surviving texts of the period.

[20] The Huguenot general François de La Noue (1531-1591), nicknamed *Bras de fer* (Iron Arm) because he replaced an arm lost at Fontenay-le-Comte in 1570 with a metallic substitute, died after being mortally wounded at Lamballe. His *Discours Politiques et Militaires* was published in 1587.

[21] Féval is speaking metaphorically here; in the 19th century, there were no commonly-agreed time-zones and the relationship between clocks in different towns was rather arbitrary, but Tours is west of Paris, so midnight—in literal terms—always arrives in Paris a few minutes earlier.

[22] Féval routinely made fun of the Germans in much the same way that he routinely made fun of the English, but his primary reference here is to the effect of German popular fiction on French fantastic fiction. When the *conte fantastique* came into vogue in periodicals in the decade before the *roman feuilleton* took off so spectacularly, its primary influence was the German writer E. T. A. Hoffmann, who was the most prestigious of a host of balladeers and storytellers fascinated by the supernatural.

German and English Gothic fiction was imitated by some of the French writers who began to write for the masses in that crucial period, including Honoré de Balzac (pseudonymously), Frédéric Soulié, the author of the classic *Les Mémoires du Diable*, and—perhaps most crucially—Etienne-Léon Lamothe-Langon. Féval joined in himself; some of his early stories were Gothic-tinted fantasies set in his native Brittany, although the ones he chose to reprint in such collections as *Contes de Bretagne* (1844) were more restrained. He certainly read Lamothe-Langon, and learned a good deal from that writer's sensationalist methods, and Soulié became something of a role-model for him, assisting him in his early ventures in the theatre.

Like Balzac, however, Féval repented his Gothic adventures even before his belated "conversion" to piety, and the first version of *La Fille du Juif Errant*, like its predecessor *Le Chevalier Ténèbre*, sets out to satirize Gothic fiction with biting mockery. Féval is however, well aware of the fact that he is exploiting the appeal of the Gothic while affecting disapproval, and employing its methods even as he decries them. His sarcastic cheers are not devoid of honest exultation.

[23] I have substituted "Stentorian" for Féval's *târteifle*, which is literally meaningless, although the latter part of it hints euphemistically at the German *teufel*, meaning Devil. When the Baron subsequently uses the word as an exclamation, I have expanded this implication.

[24] *Kiss* is what Féval actually writes; although he is crediting the word to a German speaker, he must have had the English meaning in mind.

[25] Féval has *Zâgramnete târteifle!* As with the second word, I have assumed that the phonetic implication of the first word derives from its resemblance to *sacré*, which is used purely for emphasis in association with the French *diable*.

[26] As the term *force majeure* has been incorporated into English legal jargon, I have left it as it is in the original text. It means "greater force," having originated in Roman Law as *vis major*.

[27] Charles Havas (1785-1858) founded a news agency during the reign of Louis-Philippe, which quickly became the most important in France, and remained so throughout the century.

[28] Féval's *hanneton* actually refers to another kind of bug, but cockroach fits the metaphorical meaning better in English.

[29] Féval's *la vie de polichinelle* has no exact equivalent in English, although "the life of Riley" might come close. I have preferred a more literal translation–the anti-hero of English Punch-and-Judy show being a transfiguration of the relevant character from the *commedia dell'arte*–because it probably gives a better impression of the kind of man Roland has become since being taken over by Ozer.

[30] I have used the rather quaint "wool-gathering" as the commonly sanctioned equivalent of Féval's *revient toujours de Pontoise* for want of anything better.

[31] *L'Institut de France*, a body uniting the prestigious Academies of France–literature, social sciences, sciences and arts–was founded in 1795.

[32] The reference is to the prestigious *Conservatoire des Arts et Métiers*.

[33] *The Henriade* (1723, initially as *La Ligue*; revised in 1728) was Voltaire's attempt to supply his nation with a worthy epic poem. It was widely considered to be his masterpiece at the time, although future commentators considered it a trifle cold. Its exemplary subject is the 1589 siege of Paris by the protestant Henri de Navarre, with whom the relatively tolerant Catholic King, Henri III, took refuge after being forced to flee from his own capital by the extremist League. Henri III was assassinated by a League agent, but named Henri de Navarre as his successor. Henri IV–the poem's hero–subsequently converted to Catholicism for political reasons, but maintained his predecessor's policy of tolerance. The poem uses the episode as the basis of a philosophical discussion of religious fanaticism and civil disorder, both of which Voltaire abhorred.

As he continually reminds us, Féval was not an admirer of Voltaire, or the kind of sanity of which he was the outspoken champion.

[34] The English equivalent would be confinement in the visitors' gallery of the House of Commons; the American, incarceration on the floor of the Senate.

[35] Hospodars were vassal princes of the Ottoman Empire who administered such provinces as Walachia and Moldavia.

[36] I have translated Féval's *pie-grièche* literally, although it has a double meaning in French roughly equivalent to the English "shrew," because a shrike (i.e., a butcher-bird) is a much better analogue of the kind of woman Madame Lancelot is than a harmless insectivorous mammal.

[37] When Féval wrote *La Fille du Juif Errant*, he had recently made an attempt to increase the respectability of his output with a view to putting himself forward as a candidate for the Académie Française; all the formal attempts he made failed.

[38] Chodruc-Duclos was a famous eccentric of the era; in addition to the nicknames indicated in the text, he was also known as "the modern Diogenes." He was a well-known character in and around the Palais-Royal from the 1820s to the early 1840s; although he gave every appearance of being a vagabond, he was not actually homeless, and made his way back every night–reputedly at exactly the same time–to an anonymous lodging-house in the Rue Pierre-Lescot, which is evidently the basis of the "House of Jews" Féval describes in later chapters. A year after Chodruc-Duclos died, in 1842, a volume of *Mémoires* appeared, which contained a fanciful account of his life that was almost certainly invented by some literary opportunist. It was from this volume that the sugges-

tion came that he played some deeply mysterious role in the 1830 Revolution.

[39] Prince Jules de Polignac (1780-1847) was the Prime Minister and Minister of Foreign Affairs in 1830, and was widely held to be responsible for the repressive policies that caused Charles X's downfall. He signed the ordinances of July 25 that led to the July Revolution and was imprisoned once the Revolution had been completed–not for the first time, as he and his elder brother had been complicit in the Cadoudal conspiracy against Napoleon in 1804. Féval seems unable here to forgive Polignac for having provoked the Revolution that put an end to Bourbon rule.

[40] Féval has *tron de l'aër*, which is not easily translatable; neither part of the constituent phrase is to be found in Larousse, although *tron* can still be found in English dictionaries as an obsolete term for a weighing machine used by tax-collectors and *aër* is straightforward. The reference is obviously to Polignac's repressive excesses.

[41] Yvetot is a small town northwest of Rouen. It became a principality in its own right in the late Middle Ages, answerable only to the French town. Its privileges were purely nominal by the end of the 17th century, by virtue of which it became a significant ironic symbol of "independence."

[42] This name–unlike that of the high priest Caiaphas–does not appear in the gospels (Jesus' expulsion of the merchants and money-lenders from the Temple is described very briefly in Matthew 21:12-13).

[43] Marie Minot has no entry in Larousse–nor, unsurprisingly, does the presumably fictitious Blay-le-Fossé–and is probably a literary character whose source I cannot identify. Catherine de Medici (1519-1589) married the future Henri II–then Duc

d'Orléans–in 1533. She was the mother of François II, who reigned from 1559-60; Charles IX, who reigned from 1560-74 (serving as his Regent from 1560-63); and Henri III, who reigned from 1574-89.

[44] I have not corrected the times given in the Palmé text, although the appointment was earlier made for 4 a.m., not 3 a.m.

[45] The word I have translated as "precedent" is *préjugé*, which can also mean "prejudice" or "presumption"–but Féval had once trained as a lawyer, and the first of these meanings must always have seemed primary to him.

[46] This juxtaposition is symbolic: the Val-de-Grâce had been constructed in the 17th century as a convent, but it had been transformed by the time of the July Revolution into a military hospital.

[47] Jean-Auguste-Dominique Ingres (1780-1867) was the most celebrated historical painter of his era. One of his most famous works, painted in 1832, was a portrait of Bertin, the founder of the *Journal des Débats* in the wake of Napoleon I's abolition of the Directory; he is, of course, the editor to whom Féval is referring.

[48] *Le Sire de Framboisy* (the Palmé text has "*Frambroisy*", but that is presumably a misprint) was a fake folk song composed in 1855 by Ernest Bourget and L. de Rille, when imitation Medieval music was in vogue. Féval is using it purely as an example of dissimulation, but it may be worth observing that the song describes the awful misfortunes of the eponymous character after his marriage to a much younger bride, leading to the explicitly-stated moral that "a young wife requires a young husband."

[49] *Sic transit gloria* is an abbreviation of *Sic transit gloria mundi*, from Thomas à Kempis' *The Imitation of Christ*, translatable as "Thus passes the glory of the world!"

[50] Potiphar–Féval has Putiphar–was Joseph's master, whose wife attempted unsuccessfully to seduce Joseph, and then accused him of trying to seduce her, in chapter 39 of Genesis.

[51] Holofernes–Féval has Holoferne–was a general in the army of the Babylonian King Nebuchadnezzar, featured in the apocryphal book of Judith. When he besieged the Jewish town of Bethulia, the beautiful Judith undertook to save it by unorthodox means; she seduced Holofernes, got him drunk, and cut off his head. The image of Judith brandishing the severed head became a favorite exemplar of the *femme fatale* among French writers and painters; Dumas refers to it continually while reflecting (as he frequently does) on the perfidy of womankind.

[52] Lot's two daughters committed incest with him in the wake of the destruction of Sodom and Gomorrah, as recorded in Genesis 19:30-38. There is no evidence in the Gospels that the thief Barabbas (released in preference to Jesus on the eve of the crucifixion) had a niece.

[53] Féval gives the first and last names as Coré and Abiron; only Dathan and Abiram, the sons of Eliah, were actually brothers, while Korah was the son of Levi. Together with On, the son of Peleth, the four led a rebellion against Moses (Numbers 16); the three named by Féval were swallowed up by the Earth as punishment. Although the story does not correspond to the Quran's account of Al-Sameri, which occurred at a later stage of Moses' career, it does seem to be Féval's substitute for that item in the scholars' lists of Wandering Jews.

[54] *Chocs* is the word I have translated as "conflicts"; as none of my translated lines rhyme, Chodruc-Duclos would doubtless be even more scornful of me.

[55] Féval's *Capédébiou!*, which Larousse does not recognize, might be related to the English "cap-a-pie," meaning "head to toe."

[56] Féval has *brochet*, which means "pike," but I have substituted the more general term to avoid an inconvenient double meaning.

[57] The word *centurie*, which usually refers to a company of foot-soldiers led by a Roman centurion, was adapted as the name of a set of a hundred allegedly-prophetic quatrains by the legendary Nostradamus in *Les Centuries* (1555). "Unpublished" (i.e., newly-faked) sets of quatrains turned up at regular intervals in 19th century France.

[58] A *carmagnole* was a kind of jacket favored by the Revolutionaries of 1793; the name acquired new meaning when it was adopted by a Revolutionary song, in the verse: "*Ah! ça ira, ça ira, ça ira: tous le bourgeois on les pendra.. .dansant la carmagnole.*" (Roughly, "That'll be the day, oh, that'll be the day: all the bourgeois strung up... dancing the carmagnole.")

[59] Auguste Barbier (1805-82) published a collection of satirical verses, *Iambes* (1831), in the wake of the July Revolution, denouncing those who abandoned their Republican convictions in order to take advantage of the new monarchy. Féval did not approve of Barbier's politics, but undoubtedly had some sympathy with the sentiments he expressed; it probably caused him some annoyance that in 1869 (five years after the first publication of *La Fille du Juif Errant* but before this re-

vised version appeared), Barbier was admitted to the French Academy, which persisted in refusing Féval's entry.

[60] Casimir Delavigne (1793-1843) was also a political liberal, albeit a fervently patriotic one; he was famous in his day, as much for his plays as his poetry, but is now virtually forgotten.

[61] *Boule* is the distinctively French version of bowls.

[62] This sentence translates the Latin *Q.E.D.* (*quod erat demonstrandum*) attached to proofs in mathematics.

[63] The reference to *Mère Moreau* is unclear. The context suggests that she was probably a *cabaretière*, but there is a slim possibility that she might have been the hostess of a salon–but not the poet Elise Moreau, who would have been far too young at the time.

[64] Féval is no Monsieur Galapian, but one might expect his arithmetic to be a little more consistent than this; Ozer said only a few chapters ago that he had never kept a body as long as he had kept Roland de Savray's, but this figure confirms the suggestion of his earlier remark about his birthday that he has only had 187 replacement bodies in 1,800 years (assuming that that crucifixion took place in 30 A.D. or thereabouts). Nor is Féval a would-be Nostradamus, but it may be worth observing that if we accept the implication offered here that Ozer's "lives" actually average between nine and ten years, the number of phials remaining suggests that the end of the world probably take place before 2130, most likely before 2100.

[65] The Roman Emperor Caligula gave his favorite horse, Incitatus, a furnished house and a company of slaves, presumably including the secretary mentioned here. The rumor that he appointed the animal to the Senate may be exaggerated; Sue-

tonius only reports that he is "said to have destined" a consulship for the lucky beast.

[66] The Roman Emperor Julian (331-363), dubbed the Apostate by Christians, briefly attempted to reintroduce paganism as the official religion of the fading empire–thus turning the tide against the increasingly influential Christians–after succeeding to the throne in 361. His Christian successor, Jovian, reverted to a more tolerant policy.

[67] Fredegonde was a mistress of the Frankish King Chilperic I of Neustria, who became his Queen after procuring the assassination of his wife, Galeswintha, whose more famous sister Brunhilde was the wife of Siegbert of Austrasia. Siegbert then waged war against Chilperic, beating him in battle, but was murdered in 575 by emissaries of Fredegonde. When Chilperic died, too, Fredegonde became her son's Regent and continued the war against her counterpart. Brunhilde was defeated in 596 and tortured to death, thus earning Fredegonde (who died the following year) a reputation for exceptional ruthlessness and cruelty.

[68] Philippe II (1165-1223) of France banished the Jews from his homeland. He joined the Third Crusade with Richard the Lion-Heart but withdrew from it and turned to fighting the English, annexing many of their possessions in northern France and establishing France as the leading power in Western Europe.

[69] Because they were Italian, the Medici Queens of France–Maria and Catherine—were routinely insulted by the implication that they were poisoners; the reputation was entirely unwarranted.

[70] François Ravaillac assassinated Henri IV in 1610.

[71] Louis-Dominique Cartouche (1693-1721) was the most famous French bandit of his era.

[72] Jean-Paul Marat (1744-1793) was a leading French Revolutionist, famously murdered in his bath by Charlotte Corday.

[73] A napoleon was a 20-franc piece, so five double napoleons would be 200 francs, equivalent to the promised ten *louis*–a considerable consultation fee in 1830.

[74] Mathieu Laensberg (Larousse has Matthieu Laensbergh) was a clergyman in Liège in the early 17th century. He produced the first *Almanach de Liège* in 1635 or thereabouts; it spiced up its calendrical and astronomical data with speculative weather forecasts for the year to come, prophecies of notable events and fanciful medical recipes, somewhat after the fashion of its equally persistent British equivalent, *Old Moore's Almanack*.

[75] Joseph Balsamo was, like Isaac Laquedem, the eponymous hero of a novel by Alexandre Dumas, published in 1846. The name was allegedly the original name of the pretended magician Count Cagliostro, although it may have been invented by the Roman Inquisition, which imprisoned (and presumably murdered) Cagliostro in the course of a crusade against Freemasons. Dumas made Balsamo a kind of dark messiah, destined to make war on the ruling dynasty of France on behalf of an exotic secret society derived from the Inquisition's anti-Masonic propaganda. Dumas toned down the supernatural aspects of the novel as he went along–presumably in response to editorial pressure–and by the time he got around to writing the sequel featuring the historical Cagliostro (*Le Collier de la Reine*; tr. as *The Queen's Necklace*) the quasi-messianic element had been virtually erased.

[76] The Cumaean Sibyl operated from a cave west of the modern city of Naples, some 400 years B.C.

[77] As with the reference to Joseph Balsamo, the derisive evocation of Apollonius of Tyana at this point must have been intended to make adult readers think of Alexandre Dumas, who had given such a large part to the reputed miracle-worker in *Isaac Laquedem.*

[78] *Limbes* has a double meaning in French, the more familiar being equivalent to the English "limbs"; although Féval does not give the term a capital letter, as would normally be done when the second meaning is indicated, it is clearly the other that is intended, Limbo being the neutral sector of the afterlife to which souls undeserving of Hell, Heaven or Purgatory are allegedly transmitted.

[79] Firedamp is a combustible gas formed in mines by the decomposition of coal deposits, whose fundamental constituent is methane. Mixed with air in the right proportions, it is explosive. It was a lethal hazard before the advent of the safety lamp devised by Sir Humphry Davy, which had not yet come into widespread use in 1830.

[80] The water in the pool beside which Comte Roland and Sir Arthur were laboring, when we last glimpsed them, was described, reasonably enough, as darker than the Acheron, one of the rivers of the Greek Underworld. Erebus, on the other hand, is not a river but a symbolic individual described in Hesiod's *Theogony*, one of two children (his sister Nyx is Night) of Chaos; according to Hesiod, Hemera (Day) was subsequently fathered on Nyx by Erebus, along with a further sibling, Aether.